The BLACK Stallion
and Flame

"MAY DAY, MAY DAY. This is Aircraft BAT 29167. We're almost out of gas and are being swept by hurricane winds. Exact position unknown. Come in if you hear us. . . ."

No one answered. The captain, as well as young Alec Ramsay, knew the time for ditching had come.

Yet what could they do to save the valuable cargo of horses? The only hope was to give the animals a chance to swim for their lives—but one of them was the most famous racehorse in the world, the Black Stallion!

Here is Walter Farley's thrilling story of the Black's mid-ocean separation from his devoted owner, Alec, and of the Black's adventures in a lost world of horses where, for the first time, he meets the Island Stallion, Flame!

Books by
WALTER FARLEY

The Black Stallion
The Black Stallion Returns
Son of the Black Stallion
The Island Stallion
The Black Stallion and Satan
The Black Stallion's Blood Bay Colt
The Island Stallion's Fury
The Black Stallion's Filly
The Black Stallion Revolts
The Black Stallion's Sulky Colt
The Island Stallion Races
The Black Stallion's Courage
The Black Stallion Mystery
The Black Stallion and Flame
The Black Stallion Challenged!
The Black Stallion's Ghost
The Black Stallion and the Girl
The Horse-Tamer
Man o' War

*All titles available in both paperback
and hardcover editions*

The Black Stallion

and Flame

by WALTER FARLEY

RANDOM HOUSE  NEW YORK

Copyright © 1960 by Walter Farley
All rights reserved under International and Pan-American
Copyright Conventions. Published in the United States by Random House,
Inc., New York, and simultaneously in Canada by Random House of
Canada Limited, Toronto.

Manufactured in the United States of America
Library of Congress Cataloging in Publication Data
Farley, Walter
The black stallion and Flame
New York, Random House [1960]
I.   Title   PZ10.3F22Blg   60-10029
ISBN: 0-394-80615-8 (trade hardcover)
0-394-90615-2 (library binding)
0-394-84372-X (trade paperback)

To LOUISE BONINO
editor and good friend
during twenty years of riding herd
on me and my horses

Contents

The Black Stallion
and Flame

Bat 29167

1

Like a giant bat the transatlantic plane flew through the night, using sensitive antennas to find its way. There was no beauty of flight, only a boiling turbulence that obliterated the stars high above and the sea down below. Red, white and green lights sought hopelessly to pierce the murk, blinking on and off. The four straining engines spoke loudly in defiance of the elements as driving rain pelted the plane's aluminum skin.

The wind grew stronger, spewing rain with explosive force against glass and metal. The engines labored a little more and the night grew blacker still. Suddenly the plane lurched, its wings slicing thickly through the heavy air. It righted itself and for a moment more held a steady course, then it shuddered again as if the weight of the air mass had become too great to bear. The pitch of its propellers changed, urgently straining, pounding, seeking to thrust the plane forward and upward.

The storm fought back viciously, changing rain to sleet and hail, pummeling the plane with boiling white ice and seeking to beat it down. Beneath this attack the plane was forced to descend. In the lower air there was relief from the icy blows.

But the storm did not leave it alone for long. Lightning stabbed the sky and shattered the blackness. Suddenly the plane lurched again. It was bathed in a weird light and there seemed to be a ball of fire on its nose. Propellers became whirling wheels of green vapor. What seemed like huge balloons of red, blue and green exploded everywhere in the heavens, and storm clouds took on everchanging, fiery shapes.

Directly in the center of this beautiful but frightening spectral light the plane flew unharmed. It could now be seen clearly and the name on its side read *Bermuda Atlantic Transport*. On its vertical tail fin were the large initials:

B
A
T

There was nothing soft about this plane or the men flying it. Together they'd made one hundred and twenty-six trips across the South Atlantic—from Portugal to the Cape Verde Islands, on to Trinidad, Puerto Rico, Bermuda and then, if the cargo payload warranted it, to New York.

The red linoleum floor of the flight deck heaved beneath the seats of the crew and the captain said, "A couple more jolts like the last one and we'll end up in the drink for sure." His eyes didn't leave the shaking instrument panel with its blurred figures.

Strapped in the seat to the captain's right was the copilot, his hands too on the control yoke trying to keep the plane steady. "I can take jolts better than the fire," he said. "I don't like it. I never did."

"Harmless. If all we had to worry about was St. Elmo's fire we'd be sitting fine."

"I know, but I still don't like it," the copilot said. "But, baby, just as long as the fans keep turning . . ." He didn't finish his sentence, nor did he bother to look in the direction of the propellers. There was nothing on the other side of the windows anyway but swirling darkness. The fire—a discharge of electricity combined with sleeting rain—was gone.

"She won't let us down," the captain said confidently. "Not this girl." He patted the leather crash pad above the panel. "We've been going steady too long."

For a moment the propellers bit smoothly into the night air and the plane leveled off. The needles no longer danced crazily on the green dials so the captain took one hand at a time off the control wheel and wiped his palms dry. An airman expected all kinds of weather, but nothing like this, the captain thought, without some briefing before departure. The forecaster in the Cape Verde weather room had prophesied a little light rain, headwinds of forty miles on the nose, and Trinidad clear. Nothing out of the ordinary; in fact it was quite a good forecast for the South Atlantic at this time of year. The captain had known weathermen to be wrong before but never so completely wrong as *this* one!

The plane plunged down sickeningly into an air pocket. Two pairs of hands sought urgently to pull the nose up again. Winds screamed through the antennas, propellers groaned and there was a grinding jolt as the plane hit a lower cloud bank before leveling off again.

The captain worked the controls, straining to compensate for the swirling winds. He eyed the gauges, especially the altimeter. On his next trip he'd walk into the Cape Verde weather room and tell that forecaster exactly what he thought of him! But now all he could do was to ride out this storm.

The copilot worked as hard as the captain. He advanced the throttles, keeping all four engines equal in power. *"Fans, keep turning,"* he pleaded, *"keep turning!"* They were burning over two hundred gallons of gasoline an hour. He looked at the gyrocompass, its spinning needle turning in every direction but toward their initial course. He took a second more to check the time on the black-faced panel clock. How much gas was left? And where were they anyway? It was their navigator's job to know, but the copilot was too busy to turn to him now and ask. As close as he could figure it they had fuel for about two more hours.

Suddenly the hail and lightning came on again, beating and burning the aluminum skin.

The captain's legs were numb from working the worn rubber pedals; his eyes were bloodshot from the constant strain of watching the white dancing needles on the panel; his insides groaned from the beating they were taking on this crazy, bouncing deck; and his arms felt like pieces of lead. But at least the plane was still in the air.

He pushed the nose down as engines screamed and rain whipped the windshield in a thunderous splattering of pellets. Since there was no top to this boiling mess, he'd try below again. His eyes, slits now, remained on the instruments as he ordered his copilot, "Try to raise someone again. If we don't get help soon, we'll be going for a swim."

The copilot shook his head sadly. "No night for swimming," he answered with attempted humor. The radio wires were already overheated from use and their acrid odor filled the deck, more overpowering even than the smell of high-octane gas, hydraulic oil, metal, leather and the sweat of the crew's bodies.

The copilot pressed the receivers against his ears and reached for the microphone. Twisting the dials angrily, he channeled the transmitter to route frequency, all the while knowing it would do no good. The storm static bit into his earphones. He pressed his microphone and began calling:

"*MAY DAY, MAY DAY, MAY DAY. This is*

Aircraft BAT 29167, Aircraft BAT 29167, Aircraft BAT 29167. We've run out of communications and are being swept by hurricane winds. Exact position unknown. Last position taken at 2200 was 11–14 north, 45–10 west. MAY DAY, MAY DAY, MAY DAY. Come in if you hear us. MAY DAY, MAY DAY, MAY DAY . . ."

There was nothing in his earphones but static. Finally he twisted in his seat and shot a question at the navigator, who was sitting directly behind the captain. "You got any better idea where we are?"

The navigator met the copilot's eyes. "As close as I can figure it we're going nowhere fast—just around and around."

"Funny," the copilot said bitterly, turning back to his radio and cutting off the switch.

No, not funny at all, the navigator thought. *And I didn't mean it to be, either. We've been in jams before but none as bad as this one. Our radio is out so we're deaf as well as blind. Maybe they're answering us but we can't hear them.*

He sat strapped to his stool before his navigation table. Beneath the dim light he examined his graph of position reports. There was a steady line of small x's up to the hour 2200, and then the storm had come, masking the stars with a suddenness he'd never seen equaled in all his years of flying. It had been the fastest-dropping curtain in the world. The captain had tried to get on top but because the plane wasn't pressurized, he couldn't go beyond 10,000 feet with safety and it was as thick up there as any other place.

Taped on the navigator's board beside the plotted graph were his other papers, the weather forecast and wind analysis. How could the Cape Verde forecaster have been so far off, he wondered. How could anyone have overlooked the pressures that brewed the swirling, roaring air masses of a hurricane? For that's what they were flying through; there was no doubt about it. He listened to the beating, blustering winds and rain, and wondered what name the U.S. Weather Bureau had given the storm.

A workhorse like their plane was made to ride out even hurricanes but those who guided it needed to know where they were. The navigator looked up at the astrodome of curved Plexiglas above his head. Through it he might have sighted the stars, taking a celestial fix to obtain their exact position. That is, if there were stars to sight. But there were none tonight. And without a radio he couldn't reach the transmitters of other planes and ships to take bearings upon. The failure of the radio was as strange and unpredictable as the storm itself, but such things *did* happen. Either the receiver wasn't functioning or the storm was making reception impossible.

Only loran equipment—long-range navigation equipment—could have helped him now to determine their position on his graph. But the company had decided it was too expensive to install, unnecessary was the word they used, pointing out that their planes had flown this route so many times they could almost fly it alone. The company operated on a very stringent economy program, as did most nonscheduled airlines. It had to make every ounce of payload count. The navigator knew their slogan by heart: *Economize. Save money. Save equipment. Save men*. That's why they had no separate radio operator, the job of communications being done by the copilot and the navigator. That's why they were depending upon radio telephone instead of telegraph. That's why they had no loran. That's why they were in such a jam!

Desperately the navigator bent over his board again and studied his plotted graph of position reports. He could make only a stab at figuring out their present position, and every minute he worked, another four miles of space swept by. They'd been in the air sixteen hours and fifteen minutes. He tracked as well as he could the approximate distance covered against fuel remaining and consumed. Finally he put down another small x two hundred miles off the Windward Islands of the Lesser Antilles. That was not close enough, but was the best he could do under the circumstances. He decided to keep the information to himself for the time being. No one would have believed him anyway. The spot he had marked was much too far off their scheduled course.

Suddenly the captain asked him, "How much fuel do you figure we have left?"

"Enough for another hour."

There was a greater rush of air through the ventilators, and they felt the cold touch of the storm.

"Then you'd better tell our passengers what to expect if we don't find some place to land in that time," the captain said.

"I don't have to," the navigator replied grimly. "I was with them a while ago. They're sweating it out. One old guy especially. He's had a death-grip on his seat since takeoff when there wasn't a ripple in the air."

"Get the life jackets on them anyway. Brief 'em what to do if we ditch."

"And use your most professional manner," the copilot joined in, his voice high and strained despite his attempt to be funny. "No dramatics. As the operations manual says, we must instill confidence in the passengers and make 'em believe that the crew knows exactly what's to be done. Don't ever let 'em know we're as scared as they are. It'd never do."

"That's enough," the captain ordered angrily. The soft pink and yellow lights of the flight deck disclosed the beads of perspiration on his forehead. "Stay back there with them," he told the navigator. "When I flash on the 'No Smoking' sign we'll be headed for the water. Brace yourself and hang on for good then."

The navigator unbuckled his seat belt and left his stool, the floor heaving beneath his feet. He went as far as the black curtain separating the deck from the crew cabin before turning around. "I-I guess we can't do anything about our cargo," he said.

The captain laughed grimly, and when he spoke his eyes were still glued to the instrument panel. "You've got a big heart for the company, worrying about our payload when you might be going for a swim yourself."

"I wasn't thinking about the freight. It's the rest. . . ."

"We can't do anything for sixteen thousand pounds of horses," the captain said. "They don't make life jackets that big."

The navigator parted the curtain. "I guess not," he answered, "but there's one horse in particular a lot of people are going to miss. His name is the Black and I guess he's about the most famous horse in the world. . . ."

Nightmare

2

The crew cabin on the other side of the black curtain was small, functional and very noisy since the pounding engines were only a few feet away. A coffee pot and dishes clattered in the galley and a piece of soap slithered in the wash basin. Opposite the galley were two bunks, empty except for strewn uniform caps, ties and jackets. Strapped overhead was a rolled, uninflated life raft and in a compartment beside it were three yellow life jackets.

A door opened into the passenger cabin, where most of the seats had been removed to make room for cargo. There were no smells here of high-octane gasoline or burning radio wires. Instead there were odors of hay, grain, saddle soap and leather. The dome lights beat down garishly on strong wooden box stalls holding four broodmares, eight yearling fillies and a lone black stallion.

The horses stood still, almost dozing. Except for the occasional flat, muffled explosion of a backfire, the cabin was quiet—ominously quiet.

Fear was present here, as on the flight deck. The smell of it leaked from the skin of the two men and the boy sitting in jump seats near the horses. Their faces were pale and wet with sweat, and their jaws, alternately working and clenched tight, gave further evidence of their fear. The old man grabbed the sides of his seat, his hands shaking, when the plane suddenly began to yaw and lurch. There was a sharp jolt and a quick surge of noise within the aluminum shell, then all was quiet again as the propellers found more solid air.

Alec Ramsay turned to the navigator when the crewman sat down beside him. "It's bad, isn't it?" he asked. "How bad?"

The navigator studied the boy's face a long while before answering. "I think we've ridden out the worst of it. How'd you get the horses so quiet?"

"We had to give them tranquilizer injections. They were tearing away the padding in their boxes." There were heavy circles under Alec's eyes. The muted red light on the wing went on and off, touching the boy's face—a face much too old for his age.

"What about him?" the navigator asked, nodding toward the white-haired man. "Can't you give your friend one, too?"

"Henry's all right. You needn't worry about him.

He just looks scared. I guess I'm more scared than he
is. The Black and I were in a spot like this once before.
I thought I'd forgotten it, but I haven't."

"I hope you're right," the navigator said, "and that
it was a spot something like this."

"What do you mean?"

"I mean you got out of that one."

The green navigation light at the end of the wing
blinked on and off regularly, making a tiny glow in the
darkness outside.

"You don't think our chances are very good then?"

"You want it straight or should I quote confidently
from the company manual?" It'd be better if they all
knew what they faced, the navigator decided.

"I want it straight," Alec answered. He was looking
out the window rather than at the man. The heavy
overcast had obliterated even the green light now. All
he could see was the trailing edge of the wing slicing
through the murk. It made him think of a knife slicing
through the heavy icing of a birthday cake. And that
made him think of home, when he was trying not to.

Finally he said, "What you mean is that we're going
to ditch. Is that it?"

The navigator nodded and his eyes remained on the
youth's face. "We will if we don't find some land soon.
We have gas left for less than an hour and we don't
even know where we are. Our radio communication
system has been knocked out."

"Isn't there any clear air space beneath this stuff?"

"There wasn't a while ago. No bottom. No top

either since we're not pressurized. The skipper will try again soon, I guess. You'll know when he does."

"The wind seems to have died down some."

"As I said, I think we've seen the worst of it. There's more body to the air now. She's handling better."

The big engines were no longer straining but growling in defiance of the storm.

"Maybe we'll be lucky and find something below," Alec suggested hopefully. "I-I mean something besides water."

"Maybe we will. We've been flying long enough to be over something more solid by now." The navigator unfastened his seat belt and stood up, still holding the other's gaze. He decided that whatever happened, the kid could take care of himself if given half a chance. He only hoped they'd be able to give him that much of a start. There might be waves as thick and high as mountains.

"If we do have to ditch," he went on, "it shouldn't be too bad. And our rafts will be loaded with everything we'll need until they pick us up."

Alec wanted to ask who "they" might be but didn't.

"I'll tell the others now," the navigator said, moving away.

"But what about the horses?" Alec called after him. "What can we do for them?"

The navigator turned back, a grim smile on his lips. "That's almost funny," he said. "I asked the skipper the same thing and he laughed at me—because there's nothing in this world we can do for them except hope they get a chance to swim for it."

Alec's eyes turned to Henry Dailey as the navigator went over to speak to him. He remembered Henry's words at takeoff. *"Altitude is for the birds, Alec, an' if the good Lord had meant us to fly he'd have provided us with wings. But I'll go along with you in agreein' that a night's flight to the U.S. is a lot easier on a horse than a week's trip by boat. So I'll jus' sweat this one out as I've had to do before. I won't shirk my chores but don't think for a moment I'm goin' to be good company. I'm not. I'm goin' to crawl into the shell that I've spent some sixty-odd years growin' and stay there until we land.*

"I'll be figurin' out how we might have won some of those big European classics if the Black hadn't picked up his bad stone bruise. Oh, I'm not really worried about him none. He's gallopin' all right an' I guess he could go on all day long if he had to. It's not that he's bad but he's not quite right. I want to give him a lot of time to get over his trouble. You don't take chances with this kind of horse. So I'm goin' to plan what's in store for him when he's sound again. I'll have a ball, all right, an' before I know it we'll be across the Atlantic."

Now Alec looked at his friend and wondered just how protective Henry's shell really was. It was difficult to close one's ears to the sound of the propellers and the wind screaming in the night, difficult not to listen to the uneven pounding of the engines and to ignore the severe thuds and jolts followed by the sickening drops.

Henry sat with his eyes almost closed, the perspiration on his brow oozing down the deeply etched lines of his face, and his big-knuckled hands gripping the sides of his seat.

Alec turned away, certain that Henry was prepared for any emergency even if he didn't look as if he were. One didn't ride fast horses, both on the flat and over jumps as Henry had done, without developing confidence in an ability to get out of jams.

Alec glanced at the tall black stallion, standing almost listlessly in his box a few feet away. If Alec had any protective shell like Henry's it was his horse who provided it, and he turned to him now for solace.

The strong wooden box was reinforced with metal and lined inside with straw and sack padding. Alec spoke to the Black in their secret language and the stallion raised his head, pulling against the tie-shank. The effect of the injections would last a little longer, Alec knew. It had taken two shots to quiet the Black—but without them the stallion would have battered down the sides of the box. As it was, much of the padding was strewn about the floor.

The Black closed his eyes again. He was extremely sensitive to words and sounds, including clicking of the tongue and whistling. Alec made good use of his knowledge of this, both in praise and reproach. Various pitches of his voice meant different things to the Black, and at home Alec had a secret book in which he kept the musical notes of their special language.

Even with his head down and eyes closed the tall stallion looked every bit the champion he was. His small, delicate ears were cocked forward as he dozed and the long nostrils were dilated as if to catch the slightest scent of danger. His giant body was tough yet satin-smooth. His strong legs were clean and bare of shipping bandages while bulging sinews stood out prominently beneath the skin.

The Black snored and dreamed of other nights and times, of running fresh and free. He hated to be pampered, to be bathed and washed and wrapped in blankets while his hoofs were cleaned and trimmed. Much, much better for his hide to be washed cool by strong winds and rains and warmed by many suns, and for his hoofs to be trimmed on flying rocks. He was all stallion and he knew it—strong, arrogant and cunning. Every savage instinct in him constantly sought release from the domestic life he led. Only his love for Alec and the boy's love for him kept him under control. Yet there were times like this when he dreamed of another kind of life, one he had known long ago.

Alec turned to the broodmares and yearlings. They were standing in boxes similar to the Black's, two abreast and stretching almost the whole length of the cabin. Farther aft was the rest of the cargo, most of it huge wooden crates of machinery. Everything was carefully balanced to enable the plane's big engines to conquer gravity while hauling over seventy thousand pounds across the ocean. Despite the storm none of the crates seemed to have shifted.

Alec glanced out the window. There was no break in

the heavy overcast but the winds had died as suddenly as they'd come up hours before. Perhaps the captain would find an opening below. The slight pressure in his ears told him they were descending. They might even find land. He had to think that way now. . . .

Alec turned back to the horses and to the groom who had charge of the mares. The man had unusually long arms, which hung loosely against the sides of his slight, frail body. His skin was very tanned, and he had prominent cheekbones and a long, narrow hooked nose. His appearance was not improved by an Adam's apple the size of a small red balloon, which worked continually up and down while he listened to the navigator, who had moved over beside him.

Alec sincerely hoped that the navigator would be able to convince this man that everything was going to be all right. For here was a case of somebody seeming to be paralyzed by his own fear. The groom hadn't budged in his seat for hours.

Earlier in the flight Alec had spoken to him. The man was excellent at handling horses, but he had told Alec that this job—caring for the mares and making certain they reached their destination—was only a temporary one. His charges were pure-bred Arabians being sent as a gift to a young Caribbean breeder. That was all he would say.

Alec had looked forward to meeting the new owner of these fine horses. The prospect had helped make up for the fact that he and Henry would have preferred flying a more northerly and shorter route across the

Atlantic. But air traffic was heavy at this time of year and cargo space in demand, so they had thought themselves very lucky to get space on this plane.

Leaving the groom, the navigator came forward, his face showing signs of nervous strain beneath the bright dome light. "Remove the life vests from under your seats and I'll show you how they work," he said.

Henry glanced up and grunted. "Gettin' wet feet doesn't appeal to me. Water's for washin'."

"Don't wish us into the drink before you know we have to ditch, will you?" the navigator said sharply.

"I won't," and Henry grinned feebly.

The navigator glanced out the window. "This stuff seems to be clearing. The propellers are turning smooth as silk." He lit a cigarette nervously, betraying his feigned air of confidence.

Alec motioned toward the groom, whose head was lowered as if he'd suddenly gone to sleep. "You'd better wake him up," he said.

Henry glanced back. "Imagine him bein' able to sleep with all this noise goin' on!"

"If it stops he'll wake up soon enough," the navigator said. "An engine's silence is the biggest noise there is." But he went to the groom and shook him until the man opened his eyes.

Alec listened to the even rumbling of the engines and felt a sense of great loneliness for them all. Nothing sounded wrong. If anything, the ship had suffered only minor damage in being buffeted by the storm. Nothing was wrong that some gas wouldn't help. The lack of it was the joker. The smooth, droning engines must be pulling the last of it out of the tanks.

"You'd better put your vests on now," the navigator ordered, his voice hushed, almost inaudible above the engines.

There was no sense in fooling themselves. They were all afraid. They were ready and prepared for the worst but terribly afraid. The odor of their fear filled the cabin.

"If necessary we might stretch out our run by getting rid of some of our cargo," the navigator continued. "Anything to lighten our load. It'll be up to the skipper."

Alec wiped the moisture from the palms of his hands onto the sides of his pants. He didn't dare speak. He just looked at his horse and sweated some more. No longer was he sure of himself. His red hair was wet and matted, and he wondered if he'd be able to coordinate his movements when the time came so he could get the horses clear of the sinking plane, too.

Henry slipped the life vest over his head, a sad smile on his face. "If we're going into the drink I might as well be comfortable," he said.

Alec smiled grimly at Henry's remark and put on his own vest. He straightened in his seat and told himself to remain calm. It was all right to be afraid but not to cringe.

"Remove your shoes," the navigator said, "and any sharp objects on you—pencils, pens, clips, clasps and the like. We don't want to cut any holes in the raft and, for the life of us, let's be sure to keep the horses clear of it. Their hoofs could send it down fast. It would be better to—" He paused and found Alec Ramsay's eyes upon him. "We won't leave 'em behind," he said kindly. "If we have time, we'll get them clear of the ship. Just keep them away from our raft, that's all."

The aircraft sank lower and lower into the depths of the night. There was no further turbulence. No wind screamed. No rain beat furiously against the windows. Only the heavy overcast remained and the plane sped through it, consuming time, consuming fuel. For how much longer? Was there no bottom to this murk to enable them to see what was below?

"We might not have to use these vests at all," the navigator said, "but we might as well learn how they work."

"Sure," Henry said facetiously. "We got nothin' else to do."

The navigator didn't smile. He put his arms through the loops of the vest and pulled the yellow straps tight in front. "Now there are two ways to inflate your vest," he said, "but don't do it until you're out of the ship. If you do, it'll only slow up your movements and you just might need every second to get clear."

He looked at each of them and then continued, "The first way to inflate the vest is to pull these." He tapped two plastic knobs on either side of the vest. "They automatically fill the vest by releasing capsules containing carbon dioxide. Now—"

"If that'll work why bother tellin' us about the other?" Henry asked.

"Just in case something should go wrong you can blow air into the vest through these tubes." The navigator held up the tubes. "Open this valve, turn the lock, push down the mouthpiece and blow. When you've filled the vest let go of the mouthpiece to keep the air in and turn the lock back to where it was. Nothing to it."

"Nothin' at all," Henry agreed. "But I'm not worried so much about stayin' on top of the water as I am about someone not findin' us."

"We'll use flares," the navigator said, rubbing his bloodshot eyes, "and we'll have a hand-operated radio to send out distress signals. It shouldn't be too long before somebody picks us up and, as I said before, we'll have everything aboard the raft but steaks."

Alec glanced at the groom to see how he was taking it. The man had his life vest on and seemed to have himself under better control.

"There are two main exits," the navigator continued. "This door here, the way you came aboard, and one up forward for the crew. Besides them we have eight escape windows, all plainly marked as you can see. Just remove the plastic cover from the handles, *lift up* and push. No trouble. . . ."

The plane rocked and Alec's body swayed with it. He'd been in other emergencies . . . so had his horse . . . together they'd get clear . . . some way.

The metal floor felt cold under his stockinged feet and a chill swept over him. For added warmth he pulled the life-jacket straps together in front, thinking how much like a baseball catcher's vest it was. Now if he could just convince himself that he was getting ready to play ball with the gang . . . if he could just do that and wait easily for the pitch to come . . .

The plane swayed again and Alec felt the pressure of its descent in his ears. He caught Henry watching him. "Land ho!" he yelled jokingly, not liking the sound of his voice at all.

The old man thought, *Alec's scared but not frozen stiff with fear. He'll move fast when the time comes. I just hope I can stay up with him.*

The navigator spoke again, his voice more solemn than before. "Better make sure your seat belts are tight. Take this in stride and you'll be all right."

Henry grunted, trying to get the seat belt over his heavy stomach and life jacket. "A fat chance I have to get away from the post when you've got me weighted down with so much lead. No track handicapper would be allowed . . ."

The plane broke free of the overcast and below could be seen the tossing black sea.

Angry Sea

3

The navigator went to the flight deck but returned almost immediately. "There's not much gas sloshing around at the bottom of our tanks," he told them quietly, "and no land below, so it looks like we're going to have to ditch. Just remember not to hurry. We'll have plenty of time. We'll shove one raft out this door, lower the ditching rope and drop into it. You all okay?"

Alec burrowed his head in the high collar of his life vest and swallowed hard. "Sure," he said jokingly, "except for my feet. They're cold. This floor wasn't meant for going around without shoes. I'll bet it's chilly outside."

"Now I want to tell you something else," the navigator warned. "There'll be two jolts when we ditch. The first will be kind of easy and you might get to thinking it's over—*but don't*. That's the time to brace yourself; the jolt that follows separates the men from the boys. It'll probably go dark then but don't move until I tell you to."

"Providin' we have ears to hear you with," Henry said grimly.

"Providing I'm there to yell," the navigator replied, just as grimly. "But the important thing is to keep calm and wait for the ship to come to a complete stop before moving."

"We will," Alec said. "Don't worry."

"The skipper says for us not to bother throwing anything out the hatches now," the navigator went on. "What cargo we could move wouldn't save us any fuel to speak of. It'd be meaningless in flying time and it might only upset our balance. If the skipper can bring us down under control we got a good chance . . ."

"How good?" Henry wanted to know.

"About fifty-fifty if I remember my manual figures right."

"Those aren't such bad odds," Henry said.

"Nope. The impact won't be too rough if we keep ourselves strapped. Getting out's the worst."

"How much time do we have before the cabin floods?" Alec asked.

"Depends on the sea and how we hit. Ditched land planes have been known to float hours, sometimes days."

"But they've been known to go down fast, too?"

The navigator nodded, his eyes studying the boy. He had to know whether to depend upon him or not. "As fast as three minutes," he said finally.

"How much time does the manual say it should take us to get out?" Alec persisted.

"About a minute and a half . . . ninety-six seconds, to be exact. But I think it'll take us at least two minutes. I don't know." The navigator grinned sheepishly. "I've only done this once before and that was in a swimming pool during flight training."

"I've got to get the horses free," Alec said.

"We hope to, but we might not have the time."

"I'll have to take the time," Alec said.

The navigator wiped his hands on his pants, then he pushed Alec forward in his seat. "Put your head between your legs and clasp your hands under them like this. That's it. Now tense all your muscles. There, that's the way you should be when I yell 'Brace for ditching!' You all got it?"

Alec straightened in his seat. "We've got it," he said.

"There's a packet of green dye in your life jackets just in case we get separated. It'll stain the water, making it easier to spot you from the air."

"We won't need it. We'll be in the raft with you," Henry reminded him.

"I know, but just in case—"

"Just in case nothing," Henry interrupted, trying to grin. "It's no night to be paddling around alone in the Atlantic."

The navigator moved over to the life raft and Alec looked out the window again, watching their navigation lights blink alternately like a parade of fireflies. Above them black clouds rose high and billowing but here it was quiet and safe with the plane flying smoothly through the night. Alec didn't look below at the sea's angry turmoil. It was enough to know that for a few moments they'd be given peace. The plane flew without a tremor, graceful in flight. There was no rain, no wind to impede her speed, only silence and . . .

He'd have time, according to the navigator, plenty of time . . . three whole minutes before being submerged in the sea.

Alec turned to his horse but the Black's eyes were closed in sleep. The boy kept looking at him for a long, long time while the last of the fuel flowed from the tanks to the engines.

Was this so different from their first trip together? he asked himself. If it hadn't been for a storm, the Black would never have been his. It was their ship that had gone down instead of a plane, but it was the same raging sea, the same kind of night. Was that experience to be repeated? Was he to grab hold of the Black again and be pulled to safety? Was this the beginning all over again?

Alec took his eyes off his horse, never asking himself if, instead, his life with the Black was to end where it had begun—at night, in a storm-tossed sea.

The navigator unfastened the life raft from the heavy straps which held it just aft of the main door.

They'd throw it out, inflating it with CO_2 gas to make it seaworthy . . . that would take about forty-four seconds of their precious time, he figured. A launching line would hold the raft to the aircraft while they dropped into it from the escape rope . . . depending, of course, upon how low the ship lay in the water at the time, and whether there was any need for the rope.

Alec watched the navigator, knowing that whatever happened luck would play an important part in the outcome. Air science and emergency procedures could accomplish only so much. The rest depended wholly upon circumstances. He had raced horses too long not to be well acquainted with the chances of survival in a tight situation.

He didn't think it was possible for the pilot to set the plane down under control in such a raging sea. There'd be no coming down smoothly and without a jar. They were bound to run smack into a wave, if not on first impact then soon after. It would be like hitting a brick wall, only harder, because the plane would give way beneath the force of the blow. There'd be plenty of things flying around, so *keep your head down*, he reminded himself.

Alec turned to his horse again. The worst part of it all was that there was nothing he or anyone else would be able to do during those first terrible seconds. It was a matter of prayer and luck. All one could do was to wait to find out if he was still alive when the plane stopped.

Suddenly an engine sputtered and backfired. Then another. The ship quivered, the first warning of a stall. The nose went down and the plane shook from side to side as it mushed into the lower air, its engines sputtering and backfiring violently, demanding fuel from near-drained tanks.

The "No Smoking" sign was on. The navigator called, "Brace for ditching. Hold your position until the aircraft comes to a complete stop. Be patient and orderly leaving the plane." One would have thought he was in flight-training school all over again.

Alec tensed his muscles and waited. . . .

The plane was under full control when it approached the water with just enough fuel left in the tanks to give the engines power. Slower and slower it flew, almost in a power stall . . . lower and lower like a huge bird approaching its watery nest which was now being lit by bright flares. If they were lucky the plane would make a half-decent landing and there would be little breaking up. If they were unlucky, a wing tip would hook the top of the first wave and the plane would dive straight down into the next. Now the plane swooped roughly, smoothed out again and almost stalled.

Alec's life vest was warm, comforting. He kept his head down, the collar high. He would have liked to talk to Henry or the Black during the last few seconds. His hands gripped his legs more tightly while he closed his eyes in prayer. Too bad it wasn't daylight; they would have had a better chance. There was nothing to guide them below but floating flares. *Better than nothing*, he told himself. *Better than nothing*.

An engine choked to a stop, then another, and the wind ceased whistling over the wings. The sea reached with white, foamy fingers to grasp the plane. . . .

At first it was not so different from coming down on a concrete runway, and fleetingly Alec reminded himself that he had experienced many rougher landings. But then he recalled the navigator's warning of the second jolt to come and he tightened his grip about his legs.

Then it came, and with it the frightening sounds of twisting, crumpling metal, followed quickly by the even more terrifying rush of water into the cabin. Alec felt the spray of the sea on his head! *Now! Now!* he thought, for the plane's forward movement had ceased. Cautiously he raised his head. The cabin was pitch-dark.

"Henry! Henry!" he shouted.

There was utter silence at first. Then the horses began neighing shrilly.

"Henry!" Alec called again.

This time an answer came from the darkness. "I'm okay, Alec. Twisted some but okay. You all right?"

"Yes. Can you get your seat belt loose?"

"Yeah, I got it."

A flashlight beam suddenly broke the darkness. "This way," the navigator ordered. "Watch your step. Follow the light."

The cabin was filling fast. As Alec went forward, the

water was already sloshing against his knees. The horses screamed. Some of them, Alec thought anxiously, might even be loose, their boxes shattered.

Another beam of light came from up forward and two figures, the pilot and copilot, appeared in its glow. They'd been lucky to get out of their cabin alive, Alec guessed, for the weight of the engines must already have dragged down the flight deck below water level.

The navigator called out to his crewmates, "Our tail end's been broken off. We've got maybe a minute more!" He pressed down on the heavy door handle and pushed.

Alec watched him, praying that the big door wouldn't be jammed, for only through it could they get the horses out. Luckily the door opened easily. Then the night came in with a roar, making their plight seem all the more horrible. The water line was almost level with the door; there'd be no need for the escape rope. The life raft was pushed outside, the CO_2 already filling its chambers.

The captain took hold of Alec's arm. "You first, kid," he ordered. "Get in and lie down. No standing."

"I've got to free the horses—" Alec broke away from the captain's grip and in the light from the flash he saw the shattered box stalls with the horses almost free and plunging in fear and panic. He was reaching for the Black when a hard blow landed on his jaw. His last conscious effort was that of trying to make sense out of the captain's words: "*I caught him. Now jump for it. We're going down fast!*"

The Pirate

4

The black night was almost over, its fury spent. First it surrendered to the pale gray streaks of dawn rising higher and higher into the heavens. Then came the fiery sun to pierce still greater holes in the lifting curtain.

The sea grew quiet. Shadowy waves slowly lifted and rolled forward, no longer hateful and ugly but brilliant reds and golds. A most peaceful scene, yet a lonely one, too, with nothing but the sun riding high above the now-slumbering sea.

As the great golden ball of the sun sent its rays farther and farther westward, it shone on a dark, solid object between the unbroken sea and sky.

The man-o'-war bird was all wings and it soared in the air like the great black pirate it was, seeking prey.

Then it hung motionlessly on its seven-foot wings, its forked tail trailing loosely behind. It was a somber, satanic-looking creature, better suited in appearance for night than for day. And yet it lived close to the sun, glorying in rays that turned its wings the color of glowing sable and in the air currents that lifted it higher and higher and higher. No land was in view so the ocean rover must have come a long way to be alone with the morning sun.

As it searched for something to attack, it continued to hang effortlessly in midair, its wings crooked at the shoulders and its head turning from side to side without disturbing either its buoyancy or balance. Natural instinct made it a plunderer, a hawk of the sea in search of surface life, usually fish. Its bill was long, narrow and powerful with a horny hook at the end.

For several minutes more the marine vulture hung suspended, then suddenly it swooped skillfully toward the water. It seemed to reach its goal with one stroke of its great wings, leveling off just above the sea with its long bill turned down.

Floating below was a huge blob of bright green fluorescent dye in the center of which was a tiny speck—a yellow, inflated life vest with the straps untied.

The ocean rover flew on, its powerful strokes rocking its light body, its forked tail trailing. After a short distance it stopped just above the water again with its head bent down.

A plane's wing, kept afloat by air in one of its tanks,

gleamed in the morning sun. Just beyond were several floating cushions, an oil slick and scattered pieces of wood—all that was left of BAT 29167.

The man-o'-war bird rose into the heavens and began circling. Higher and higher it soared as if following the air paths to the very sun itself. It seemed to be little more than a black sail in the sky when its head stopped turning from side to side and its eyes became fixed on a small, bobbing object in the distance.

An occupied life raft rode gently on the rolling sea.

Henry Dailey pulled his life vest closer about him and looked skyward. "I'm glad to see the sun," he said to no one in particular. "For a while I thought I wouldn't." He turned to Alec, putting his hand on the boy's shoulder. "The Black's a good swimmer, Alec. Don't worry about him none."

The navigator spoke up. "I wish that groom could've swum a little. He fell off the wing when the raft slipped away from us. I still thought he'd make it but his straps must have come loose. He went down and didn't come up."

The captain said, "You've told us all that before. Stop blaming yourself. You did what you could for him in the time we had. We all did . . . and we're still a long way from being safe."

"Sea-Air Rescue must have been alerted by now," the navigator said a little desperately.

"Don't sound so grim, ol' buddies," the copilot said.

"We're long overdue," the navigator went on, even more urgently than before. "*Somebody* oughta have missed us by now."

Alec lifted his face; it was that of an old man, tired and beaten. "You're sure . . . you're sure the Black didn't go down with the plane?" he asked Henry again.

The trainer nodded his head. "I'm sure. All the horses got clear right after we did; that's what cut the raft loose from the ship. One of them got caught in the launching line and broke it."

"You saw the Black? You're sure?"

"He was right there with them. An' I saw him again a minute later when they started swimmin'. We had to keep them away from the raft so their hoofs wouldn't tear it wide open."

"That . . . that was the last time you saw him?" Alec asked.

Henry nodded again. In the rough sea he'd been lucky to see the horses at all, but he wasn't going to tell Alec that. It was enough that only one human life had been lost . . . so far. As the captain had said, they were still a long way from being safe. Henry turned to the copilot, who was letting out a small hydrogen balloon to which a radio antenna was attached.

The crewman caught Henry's gaze and smiled grimly. "This is a friend of mine," he said, patting the small but compact radio transmitter at his side. "It's called the Gibson Girl. Maybe you know the reason better'n I do, hey ol' buddy?"

Henry tried to smile. "Yes, I guess I do," he said, his eyes finding the curved waterproof case. "It has something to do with her lines."

"Anyway," the copilot went on, "she's a very remarkable little girl. We'll crank her up an' our SOS will be heard for more than a hundred miles. Any ship or plane will be able to take a bearing on it."

"If there *are* any ships or planes within a hundred miles," the navigator pointed out.

"Ol' happy buddy, buddy," the copilot said. "Making us feel real good about everything this morning, aren't you?"

"Cut it out you two," the captain ordered. "Anyone hungry?"

They all shook their heads.

"Just as well, I guess," the captain continued. "We'd better go easy on our emergency rations. It might be a long time before we're picked up."

"At least we're going to get dry," Henry said, turning again to the sun. "It was so cold there for a while. . . ."

"I just hope it doesn't get *too* warm for us," the captain said, his gaze following Henry's. "We've got to be very, very careful with our drinking water."

"Water, water everywhere and not—" the copilot recited until stopped by the captain's eyes. A cloud drifting across the sun cast a shadow over the small raft and suddenly the cool air felt very damp and penetrating.

The copilot tried all over again. "Well, what I meant

is that now all we have to do is *wait*." He wiped his hands on his pants and began cranking the Gibson Girl.

Henry's gaze remained skyward. There was a big bird up there; for a moment he'd thought it was a plane. Might be a good omen at that . . . a bird had to have a nest on land, didn't it? Maybe if they were real lucky they'd find its home. But for now, as the copilot had said, all they could do was to wait . . . and, Henry added to himself, *to pray*.

The man-o'-war bird did not swoop to the sea to investigate the life raft. After hovering high over it for several minutes, it flew on. Far to the west it traveled before dipping lower and lower and lower toward the sea. Finally it hung motionless not more than a hundred feet above the water.

Below swam a small group of horses.

The Black, leading the band, was very tired. And he was afraid. Water was not his element and he'd spent terrifying hours in the darkness fighting to stay afloat in a cold and high-running sea. Only when the black night had been broken by pale gray streaks of dawn had he taken heart. But with the morning had come, too, an overwhelming sense of loneliness. He neighed repeatedly, looking for the one he loved, and swam on trying to find him. But no familiar scent filled his nostrils—only the odors of the sea, iodine and salt.

The waves lifted him high, then swept him down

into deep troughs with walls of water closing out the gray dawn. The sun rose, a pale disk scattering isolated patches of fog until they looked like flimsy veils hanging close to the sea. As the Black felt the pull of currents on his body, instinct told him not to fight them. He let them take him where they would. The soft wind blew persistently, its warm breath soothing. The water, too, grew warm, slowly becoming an indigo blue. For the first time the Black felt a strong surge of hope stir within him. He had entered a "river" in the sea and he let the fresh, strong current carry him on, his long legs moving only enough to keep him afloat.

He was aware of the huge bird above him but he ignored it, instinct telling him that he had nothing to fear from it. His enemies were below, deep in the water where he could not see them. A short distance away the sea suddenly boiled with little fish, leaping and splashing, their bodies silver in the sun. They were not playing, he knew, but struggling to survive. What was going on below the surface to scare them so? Whatever it was, he, too, feared it.

The man-o'-war bird continued to hang motionless in the air.

A dorsal fin and tail knifed the blue water, wove gracefully in and out, then disappeared below. A few minutes later the big fish rose again, this time leaping clear of the sea in a long graceful arc, its body a lustrous blue and silver in the morning light. It was a marlin, and it must have eaten its fill, for when it submerged again the boiling waters became still.

Yet the Black knew that a choice between life and death remained, and that there was no time to rest. He watched the sea about him for strange shapes that could only be dangerous, fierce and horrible because he had little means of fighting back. Suddenly two monstrous eyes stared at him from a few feet away. He kicked out savagely, and the eyes and snout in the big forepart of the creature disappeared below, its tentacles clawing the air. The giant squid skidded away.

The broodmares and fillies swam closer to the Black, and he looked up at the big bird hovering alongside, wondering why it remained. His gaze returned to the sea around him but his ears stayed cocked in the bird's direction as he listened to sounds inaudible to the human ear. The other horses, too, pointed their ears in the bird's direction.

The man-o'-war bird suddenly began moving its wings, flying higher into the sky. It gave one shrill call, then was quiet again except for the beating of its tremendous wings. After a short while it was no more than a black sail in the heavens, circling and rising with the upper winds.

For many hours the strong ocean current carried the Black and his small band to the north and west. By mid-afternoon they were joined by hundreds of swarming birds and the scent of land was strong! The Black watched the birds, some peeling off from formations and diving into the sea after fish while others drifted and soared, waiting to steal.

Flying fish streamed by in a procession of silvery bodies. They zipped magically out of the water and glided long distances before dipping their tails into the sea and rising again. When they finally came down, they skittered along the surface before plunging into the depths.

Close to the Black a pelican rested after its plunge into the sea from lofty heights. It threw back its heavy-billed head and swallowed its catch. A floating cormorant beside the pelican stretched its long neck and violently beat the air with its wings, then it dived below in search of food. Busier than any of the other birds were the small terns, fishing endlessly and seemingly without rest. They struck the water again and again and again, emerging immediately always against the wind, a fish in their bills, and seeking to keep and eat it before losing it to a pirate gull.

An hour before sunset the homeward flight of the birds began. Except for the pelicans, who appeared to be content to spend the night at sea, they streaked for roosting places on distant reefs.

The Black made no attempt to break away from the warm current and follow the birds. He let himself be borne along as they and, later, the reefs slipped by. And all the while he kept looking toward the west. His eyes strayed only occasionally, and each time it was to glance skyward at the black bird still flying high above.

Still later, a familiar scent grew strong in his nostrils and a short distance away the cloudy peak of an island rose from the sea. It was bare of vegetation and seemed more foreboding than the tiniest coral atoll he had passed.

Hovering in the wind above this island peak was the man-o'-war bird. Below in an isolated nest was another of its kind, a female with brownish-black feathers and a splotched white breast. Standing erect beside her was a young creature of the same species, completely white except for black wings like its father's.

The man-o'-war bird suddenly folded its wings and swooped down. For the first time a small pouch of red skin beneath its neck was visible. As the bird neared home this pouch became inflated like a toy balloon.

Safe Haven

5

The Black Stallion's nostrils quivered as he swam upwind, approaching the island with what seemed to be a strong homing instinct. If what he smelled was frightening, he showed no outward fear. But he kept his ears pointed landward as he listened for sounds carried on the wind. He swam faster, snorting repeatedly.

With strong herd instinct the mares followed him. They had accepted their leader without question and now they listened to his snorts warning them of immediate peril in the waters directly ahead. It was important that they remain close together in times of danger.

Shadows of a coral reef appeared below the surface, some sections of it rising higher than others and breaking the surface. Hoofs and legs could easily be broken on such a barrier. Blue waters churned white as they washed over the rock, becoming black as the sea deepened and waves gained momentum, crashing hard against the island's formidable walls.

It was a strange island, unlike any other in the Caribbean Sea. There was nothing green or tropical about it, nothing luxurious or colorful. It rose out of the turquoise blue waters with a bleakness that seemed to forebode evil and death to those who would attempt to approach it. From the sea it looked like a massive, egg-shaped boulder completely devoid of life, its sheer, bare sides looming from the thin veil of gray mist that shrouded its base. The walls towered to a height of a thousand or more feet, rounding off to form a dome-shaped top that gleamed in the setting sun.

The Black Stallion carefully led his band across the reef. He hated the sea and was tempted to swim faster, leaving it behind him forever. He wanted to feel again the earth beneath his hoofs. But he didn't move his legs faster; instinct told him that the submerged coral lay all about.

Snorting, he changed course again, choosing his way more carefully than before. He continued swimming toward the island, the mares following him almost in single file. His eyes shifted constantly, leaving the waters for the barrier wall that was stopping the sea in its tracks. He scented the air and changed course once more.

When he reached deeper water, the height and momentum of the swells carried him forward at ever-greater speed. He sought to check himself, churning his legs and bringing his strength and weight to bear against the sea. He managed to keep off the crest of some waves by fighting his way through them and sliding into deep troughs. Slowly but ever so surely he neared the great wall of stone.

Snorting shrilly, he sought to keep his head above a giant wave but the furious waters washed over him despite all he could do. When he came to the surface he snorted again and his eyes sought the bobbing heads of the frantic mares. Ahead of them loomed the sheer wall, ceaselessly being struck by the climbing spray of the sea.

The waters swirled about the Black Stallion and poured over his head. Yet his eyes and nostrils were never still and finally he swam eagerly toward a *low but wide hole in the wall!* It was just high enough to accommodate his body and once through he was able to raise his head high.

The chamber inside, which had a sandy floor, was very large with a canal running through the center. On either side were moss-covered piles of petrified wood centuries old. Only the light coming through from the sea illuminated the chamber but it was enough to disclose that there were manure droppings in the sand.

The Black Stallion climbed out of the canal, whinnying to the mares to follow. His nostrils were dilated, his ears cocked. He stood still for a moment, awaiting his band. The only thing about him that moved was his mane, stirred by the wind that found its way through the hole in gusts.

When all the broodmares and fillies had climbed out of the canal, the Black led them past rock to the far corner of the chamber. There he stopped, waiting for his eyes to become accustomed to the darkness beyond. It took several minutes before he could see well but he did not shy or appear to be startled by what he saw. Without hesitation he went into one of several long tunnels that opened off the chamber. As he picked his way along, he favored his bruised foot, for the path was stony.

It wasn't long before he no longer felt the gusts of wind at his back or heard the dull thuds of the waves striking the outer wall. Eventually he emerged from the tunnel and led the mares through a long chasm. Sheer cliffs rose on either side and the open sky of early evening could be seen above.

The chasm opened into a small sliver of a valley with a stream crossing its center. The stallion lengthened his strides, running to the fresh water to drink his fill. And in that valley he and his small band spent the night.

The mares' need for each other was great and they grazed in a closely knit group as if afraid to wander away alone more than a few feet. But even within the group each mare had her special attachment, pairing off usually with the one who had been stabled closest to her on the plane. They stood head to flank, their tails whisking the night air, their teeth cutting the grass. They could eat in peace, knowing that their leader was on guard and looking out for them. Some of them even lay down and slept in the early hours. Soon others followed suit, and finally only the Black Stallion was left standing to keep his lonely vigil.

The Black made no sound, not even chopping the grass with his sharp teeth. He listened to the night wind racing across jagged rock. He smelled all it carried, his nostrils never still.

A full moon rose in the night sky, its light enhancing the solemn beauty and solitude of the small valley. Finally the stallion relaxed his vigilance and bent his long, graceful neck down to the grass. But a little later he raised his head again, his nostrils quivering. Not a muscle moved beneath his velvet-soft coat. Sensing danger, he remained very still, every sense alert. For many minutes he remained that way. Then, as suddenly as the scent had come, it was gone. The Black's bulging muscles relaxed. Once more he grazed.

Early dawn found him on the move, taking his band to the far end of the narrow valley and down a deep gorge. It was a dry stream bed, strewn with sharp rocks and boulders. The Black went slowly, following the twisting trail and favoring his bruised foot again. Yet even over this rough terrain his action was free and graceful, and his eagerness to run was apparent in every stride.

He emerged from the gorge to enter a low marshland into which the stream must once have emptied. A thin cloud of vapor was rising from the hollow and with it came the added warmth of early morning. The Black Stallion brought his band to an immediate stop, the foul smell of rotting vegetation strong in his nostrils. He whirled and shook his head as if undecided about going on. Pawing the ground, he found it too soft and not to his liking at all.

He snorted to the mares, warning them of their danger. His tail swished angrily and suddenly he swung his hindquarters around, lashing out at a reluctant filly. He snorted to another, lifting his forefeet and stomping the ground repeatedly. Finally he had them all in line and whinnied his command. He led them forward in single file, carefully choosing a path through the swamp.

Their bodies were shrouded by the clinging gray veil of mist. On either side of the narrow green path over which they passed were high reeds and swamp ferns. There too lay quicksand which would have engulfed their bodies within a few minutes' time and left no trace. A slip, a fall, and horrible death awaited each and every one.

The Black moved at an ever-faster pace through the cloudlike world, his hoofs making soft sucking noises. He was anxious to get clear of the marsh. And to lend wings to his feet were other hoofprints in the path before him!

Suddenly the route led upward, taking him away

from the hollow. In his mounting excitement he broke
into a hard run and left the mares behind. Reaching
the top of the incline, he entered a large field of wild
sugar cane. Beyond it, stretching the length of the
island, was an open valley. It was like a blue-green
jewel set deep amid towering walls that were the color
of pure gold.

The morning light found its way into the valley
through a long, narrow crack that split the dome of the
island. At the upper end of the valley an underground
stream wound its way from the blackness of a huge
cavern into the open, then dropped in a shimmering
sheet of white to a pool two hundred or more feet
below.

The Black Stallion came to a stop and screamed his
high-pitched clarion call, claiming this new land for
his very own. The air rang with his challenge,
vibrating from wall to wall. And when his call finally
died the morning stillness was broken once more.

Drinking at the pool was a great herd of horses.
From it a tall chestnut stallion stepped forth, his head
held high, his eyes defiant as he turned downwind.
Like the Black Stallion's, his head was small with
prominent, ever-watchful eyes. Great muscles bulged
beneath his sleek, battle-scarred coat. He screamed
his answer and it was as savage and wild a call as the
Black's!

The valley was no longer peaceful. It had become a
walled arena.

Survival

6

At the time of the stallions' meeting—one hour after dawn on the second morning at sea—Alec Ramsay awakened. With the others he was huddled on the floor of the raft and covered by a tarpaulin. The night had been cool and the extra canvas felt good. Another tarpaulin was rigged overhead to collect dew and to be used later as a sunshade.

He shifted, straightening the canvas beneath him. It was still dry and warm. To restore circulation he moved his shoulder and back muscles, then leaned forward, flexing his fingers and toes. He shivered slightly and stopped doing the mild exercise to warm his hands beneath his armpits.

There might not be any sun that day, for the morning sky was cloudy. And if it rained, well, at least it would provide drinking water. He raised his feet slightly and held them up for a moment or two. Then he grimaced a couple of times, working his facial muscles, too. That done, he made sure his socks were pulled well up over his trousers and that his sleeves were rolled down as far as they could go. He pulled down the wide-brimmed hat that the captain had given him and put on his sunglasses. Even on cloudy days the sun could give one a severe burn.

He thought only of survival. He couldn't, wouldn't think of his horse. Later maybe, but not now.

They might be picked up today—or not for days or weeks. Emergency rations and water were limited. They would be limited to less than a quart of water daily, the captain had told them. And the best foods to eat were those with high carbohydrate content, such as hard candy and fruit bars.

Alec stretched out, resting again as the others were doing. Activity meant they would require more food and water, so the less they did the less nourishment their bodies would need. He moved more of himself under the sunshade, for the sun had just peeped from behind the clouds. Even to look at it made him very thirsty. Water was his most important need. With it alone he'd be able to live ten days, maybe longer, because his will to live was very strong.

Relax and sleep, he told himself. *The less you think about water the better. We have a sun-still and a de-salting kit. Besides, it's going to rain. We're well off. We're in good shape.*

The motion of the raft made him a little dizzy, even sick to his stomach. He tried to ignore it. He didn't want to lose what little food he'd eaten. He watched the clouds, waiting and ready for a shower to descend. But the sun kept shining more brightly, piercing the cloud deck more often. It might, after all, be another scorcher like yesterday. He'd have to stay beneath the shade except when he dampened his clothes during the hottest part of the day; that would cut down the amount of water he lost by sweating.

It was the night that was most welcome, when they could move about without fear of the sun and try to catch some fish. Even though the fishing kits had been lost with the plane, they had improvised hooks from the crew's insignia pins. For cord they'd used threads from their clothes. They had found small fish gathered beneath their raft. Larger fish had been attracted by shining a flashlight onto the water. They'd speared some of them by lashing a knife to an oar. But the best catch of all was a flying fish that had landed in the raft.

They had cleaned and eaten it immediately, giving it no chance to spoil. Alec wondered what his mother and father would have thought of his eating *raw* fish and wishing for more! He rubbed sunburn cream over his face, a face no longer young but lined and grim. Was his horse already dead? Why did these things have to happen? All he could do was to lie still, to wait, to agonize. . . .

Henry Dailey still slept, too tired to move, too old to care. But the captain, who had been sleeping alongside Alec, sat up, glanced at the sun and shook his head sadly. So far he'd done all he could, everything according to the rules and the book. He had checked the physical condition of all on board and they were in as good shape as could be expected. Tomorrow and the next day and the one after that might tell another story. But he'd face that when he had to.

He had planned on one good meal daily; two would have been preferable but they didn't have enough food in their survival kits to last if they were adrift more than a few days. The food in the kits had been carefully chosen to provide proper sustenance in just such cases as this, and if they could catch enough seafood to go along with it they could survive even longer when the food in the kits was gone. Water was even more important for their existence. He had figured they could get by on less than a quart daily. He had set up their sun-still and de-salting kit and he counted on getting more fresh water by collecting some rain and dew.

The compasses, watches, matches and lighters were being kept in dry, waterproof containers. He was keeping his log, indicating time of ditching, winds, weather, direction of swells, time of sunrise and sunset and other navigation data. He had remained calm, setting an example for the others. He'd even laughed and gotten the others to do likewise. He had salvaged from the plane's debris extra clothing, Thermos jugs and cushions.

He had made sure the raft was properly inflated.
The air chambers were well rounded but not drum
tight. They needed checking constantly. Air expanded
on hot days so he must remember to release some
during the day and add air at night when the weather
cooled. And he must remember to keep that valve
tight.

He had improvised a sea anchor, too, by using a
drag from a raft case. The closer they remained to the
ditching area the better chance they had of being
picked up—or so he liked to believe.

He had checked the raft constantly for leaks,
examining all valves and seams and underwater
surfaces, then wrapping the anchor rope with cloth to
make certain it wouldn't chafe the raft. He made sure
all aboard were careful with their fishhooks, knives
and ration tins. He never allowed them to put such
things on the floor. He kept the raft properly balanced, making the heaviest person sit in the center.
He had repair plugs for use if necessary.

He knew Sea-Air Rescue would be looking for them
by now. The message to all ships and planes in the
South Atlantic would have read something like this:
*Urgent. All aircraft and ships are requested to be on
the alert for survivors and distress frequencies from
Bermuda Atlantic Transport 29167 unreported since
2200. Last reported position 11–14 north, 45–10
west. . . .*

He had received similar messages himself in the
past and twice had been successful in helping to locate

the survivors of ditched planes. He glanced skyward. It was comforting to know that somebody was up there looking for them. He'd have to help in every way he could, for a raft in the open sea could easily be missed if those on it didn't cooperate with the searchers. When he saw a plane he'd use mirrors and every other possible signal device to let it be known they were down here. Although it was summer, it could be awfully cold sitting on a raft in the open sea. And lonesome. Yes, it was nice to know somebody was up there looking for them . . . just as he had done for others and would do again providing he lived through this.

The copilot's thoughts were similar to the captain's. His eyes scanned the sea, noting the whitecaps and the shadows of the scattered clouds. It was touch and go between rain and sun. Which would it be? He picked the sun and hoped he was wrong. The search area had to be a great one and how would high-flying planes ever be able to spot an object as small as their raft?

During the storm they had been out of communication range for too many hours to give their searchers a clue as to where they had ditched. He looked up at the small hydrogen balloon that carried their radio antenna aloft. Their SOS would let their searchers know they were still alive and awaiting help. But were they getting through to anyone?

He kept turning the hand-energized transmitter,

sending out the SOS steadily. And, like the captain, he held a mirror in his hand, flashing it in the sun. Aircraft would see the flashes long before those below could see or hear the plane.

When help appeared they'd send off their smoke signals or, if it happened to be nighttime, their red signals. The flares were being kept dry and ready just in case. Then too they had their green sea-marker for daytime use and their flashlights for use at night. Now all he had to do was to relax—and keep cranking, of course. Keep sending out that SOS . . . SOS . . . SOS. . . .

The navigator had his own separate thoughts. He figured, *I'd estimate our position to be 17–30 north, 57–30 west. That puts us in touch with the Windward Islands where we ought to be able to land.* He passed on the estimated position to the captain, who put it immediately in the log.

The night had enabled the navigator to lose his sense of helplessness; the weather had been clear and ideal for sighting the stars. He'd had no trouble. Using his automatic octant he'd shot Pollux, then plotted and calculated their position on his chart. Just before dawn he'd been able to get a good three-star fix and was confident that their position was more or less correct. He took up a compass heading of 114 degrees and figured it shouldn't be too long before they sighted one of the islands.

He sat up and, just to make sure, shot several

single-shot sun lines, then crossed a line and a radio
bearing for a fix. He studied coordinates. Yes, he still
made it 17–30 north, 57–30 west. If he was right, the
island of Antago should be showing up in the west any
time now. But just in case he was wrong, he'd better
keep that information to himself. Surprises were
easier to take than disappointments.

It didn't rain. The shadows of the clouds on the sea
became more scattered. The sun beat down on the raft
and the long hours went by slower and slower and
slower. Even the fish seemed to seek refuge from the
sun by gathering underneath the shadow of the
bobbing raft.

The captain was on watch and now he stirred
beneath the protection of the tarpaulin to pick up his
insignia pin. He opened it carefully to avoid putting a
hole in the raft, tied a parachute shroud line to it and
then dropped it into the water. Before long a fish
struck the shiny pin. After killing it with a blow on the
head the captain pulled it eagerly aboard, careful to
keep the fish's spine from touching the inflated
rubber. Then he turned to the others, wanting to
share his catch with them.

They were all asleep and he didn't want to wake
them. Sleep was most important. He decided to keep
the fish intact until they awakened. He secured it to
the side of the raft, letting it trail deep in the water to
keep it away from the sun.

A moment later he realized that he had made a

terrible mistake. Not more than a hundred yards away from the raft a dorsal fin split the blue water like a huge black sickle. Then it was gone, the shark plunging down deep below the surface with a great splash of his tail fin.

Had it gone or was it after the bait? The captain reached for the line trailing in the water. Now he remembered the warning in his operations and survival manual! *"Avoid attracting or annoying sharks. Most of them are scavengers continually on the move for food. If they don't get it from you they will lose interest and swim on. Don't fish from your raft if sharks are nearby. Abandon hooked fish if shark approaches."*

The captain didn't call the others. He sat alone, stonily silent, waiting . . . pulling the line in as fast as he could. Then the huge dorsal fin broke the surface again and he could have touched the shark. Breathlessly, he waited. The line snapped and his fish was gone.

The captain pulled in the cord and sat back, praying he'd seen the last of the shark who could so easily slash the rubber raft and sink it.

He wondered how ferocious sharks really were. Some people said that unless driven to fury sharks were usually harmless; others maintained they were willing to eat anything that came within reach. *Quiet now*, the captain told himself. *Don't move. Maybe he's gone away.*

But the shark reappeared, swimming around the

raft, his dorsal fin raised high. Again and again he circled, coming so close that the captain scarcely dared to breathe. Would the shark charge? Would he make a quick pass at the raft?

The captain watched, not daring to move. He counted the number of times the shark circled the raft. He considered calling the others but decided to put it off for another few seconds. He was scared. He picked up an oar.

The shark whipped the water with his tail and disappeared below again. Where would he come up now? Beneath the raft?

It was time to call the others, quickly! But before the captain could make a move the dorsal fin broke the surface more than fifty feet away. The captain breathed easier. *Get out of here, you. Get!* he almost screamed aloud. His hands tightened about the oar.

Suddenly the shark turned and twisted completely around, streaking directly for the raft! The huge dark fin cut through the sea of glass, leaving whorls of ripples behind.

The captain struck the water with the flat of the oar, hoping the noise would scare the shark away. The sharp retort shattered the quiet and the others in the raft sat up abruptly as though they had been struck in the face.

"Look sharp, everybody!" the captain ordered. "A shark's after us. He's somewhere right around us but he won't stay down long."

The captain's voice snapped them to attention, and

they strained their eyes trying to pierce the depths. *Oh, good Lord, don't let him come up beneath us!* they thought as one. *Not that!*

"There's something off to starboard. Is that it?" the navigator shouted. "No. No. Nothing. Look to port. There. No, it's another shadow."

"Quiet!" the captain ordered sharply.

They all saw the fin far off to one side. Maybe their enemy was leaving. They scarcely breathed. It was the biggest dorsal fin any of them had ever seen. The shark must have been thirty or forty feet long from dorsal fin to tail! All he had to do was to lunge at them just once, to hit and run—and it would be the end. The shark seemed to have stopped momentarily, lying just beneath the surface. Was he resting, waiting? Would he attack or wouldn't he?

"He'll leave. I know he will," Alec said.

"I hope so," the navigator responded fervently.

"If he doesn't—"

"Smile, ol' buddies. We're still afloat," the copilot said grimly.

"Quiet!" the captain ordered.

"There he goes—down again," Alec said.

They waited, sweating from fear that the raft might suddenly rise beneath them. But nothing happened and that was the last they saw of the huge black dorsal fin.

Despite its sea anchor, the raft had moved with the wind and current. In the early afternoon the captain took in the sea anchor and rigged a square sail in the bow, using tarpaulin, and oars as mast and crossbar. He erected the mast by tying it securely to the front cross seat and providing braces. He padded the bottom of the mast to prevent it from chafing or punching a hole in the rubber floor. For a rudder he used an oar. "Now," he told the others, "let's try to get someplace. It doesn't seem that anyone's looking for us."

"We haven't reached anyone, that's why," the copilot said, still cranking the Gibson Girl.

"I think we've got a pretty good chance of finding something," the navigator told them for the first time. "According to my estimate . . ."

Their eyes turned to him, pleading and hopeful. "I could be wrong," he went on. "Don't get all steamed up. But there's a chance, a good one, that we might sight land today. Keep looking."

The late afternoon sky was clear except for a strange cloud that hovered close to the sea. The atmosphere there had more of a greenish tint than the area around it—as if, perhaps, it was a reflection of sunlight from shallow lagoons or shelves of coral reefs. All the rest of the sea was either dark green or dark blue, indicating deep water.

The crew watched the hovering cloud. Might it not mean that land was near? Didn't the survival manual state that sometimes such a cloud in a clear sky hangs over or floats downwind from an island?

They sniffed the air for smells of land which would carry a long way over the sea with the right wind.

They hoped to smell the musty odor of mangrove swamps and mud flats, and that of burning wood. They listened for the roar of the surf and the cries of sea birds that might already be roosting on some nearby land. Their eyes searched the skies for birds flying homeward at dusk. Finally they saw a flock far in the distance, a long file making a beeline for the center of the hovering cloud! They watched the flowing stream of birds in dead silence, afraid to speak, even to hope, able only to pray. They watched so intently that each and every one thought he could actually hear the soft, humming swish of wings and, below the birds, the roar of the surf breaking on an island shore.

After a long while the captain shifted his gaze from the cloud and studied the sea. There was no doubt that the pattern of the waves was changing. He turned to the others, saying quietly, "I think it's safe to say we're approaching land."

"If it's land, it's the island of Antago, according to my reckoning, the most windward of the Lower Antilles," the navigator said.

"I don't care what it is, ol' buddy, just as long as it's solid ground," the copilot answered.

"You'd better care," the navigator retorted. "Why be stranded on a deserted island? Antago's got people, plenty of them, and ships to take us *home*."

The wind was strong on their quarter as they sailed westward, and by sunset they were within sight of land. It rose from the sea in a series of rolling hills of green cane rimmed by palm-fringed beaches. But more heartening to the survivors than the beauty of the land were the villages rising from the waterfront to high, well-cultivated plains. There was nothing remote or primitive about the island; it was productive, civilized, a place where they could easily get help.

The rays of the setting sun shone in the captain's eyes as he tried to select his landing point carefully. He watched for gaps in the surf line and headed for them. He ordered everybody to put on life vests again and trailed the sea anchor over the stern with as much line as he had. The anchor together with the oars would help keep the raft pointing toward shore. If possible they'd ride in on the crest of a wave. He didn't expect any trouble. It was only a medium surf with a small coral reef to cross. They had won! They had staved off death. They were going *home*. It was good to think about. He had a wife and four kids.

"It won't be long now," he said aloud but softly.

They were all nodding quietly back at him, all but the boy Alec, who wanted with all his heart to know the answer to the question that tormented him: *I wonder if my horse made it too?*

Walled Arena

7

The chestnut stallion stood motionless on a slight incline overlooking his herd. He might have been a giant statue on a pedestal except that no sculptor could have reproduced accurately his fineness of form and carriage.

He was the color of fire and the very air about him crackled as if he were discharging invisible flames. His head was small but his eyes were large and black and brilliant. It was his eyes that betrayed him for what he was—a wild stallion on guard, alert, questioning and dangerous.

Suddenly, and for the first time in many minutes, he moved. There was a quivering of his flaring nostrils, followed by a nervous twitching of his ears. His cascading mane and tail were picked up and riffled by a sudden gust of wind, then he was still again.

He was the veteran of hundreds of battles, completely unafraid of the intruder who sought his mares as openly as this black one. He raised his handsome head higher, surveying the stranger's small band and coveting it. His body rocked slightly on his long, clean legs, and the interplay of his muscles was beautiful to see. He exuded power, bearing himself as if he could never be conquered by man or beast, never be ridden or put between shafts. And he knew exactly what to do in the face of danger.

He turned to his own mares, moving with all the dignity of a thousand monarchs. He was the object of trembling reverence and awe until he snorted. Then the mares heeled like a giant pinwheel, starting to form a tight circle with their hindquarters at the outer edge. Mindful of their long-legged foals at their sides, some of the mares trotted more slowly than others. The red stallion moved upon them swiftly. Nipping the tardy mares gently, for he was considerate as well as intelligent, he hurried them into formation and then turned again to face his foe. He waited for the fight to be brought to him.

The moments dragged on. He waited for the strange stallion to move, to fidget. But it seemed that his foe, too, was content to wait. Such steadiness in another stallion was unknown to him. In all his years of combat it had never happened before. Little did he know that the strange stallion was his equal in all things and that he faced the fiercest battle of his life.

The Black Stallion wasn't startled by what he had found. The trail he had followed was plainly marked with hoofprints as large as his own, and the scent of other horses had been strong in his nostrils. But now he did not go forward eagerly. He quieted his excited mares with a sharp reprimand and then stood stock-still while the breeze bent the tall cane around them.

Only the rapid rise and fall of his ribs and the brightness of his eyes betrayed his excitement. He began to breathe harder, his strong muscles bulging beneath his glossy satin coat.

His eyes left the leader of the herd just once. That was when he glanced skyward at the flowing clouds and saw the great black bird that swept across the valley and perched itself on a dead tree beyond the cane.

The Black turned back to his foe, waiting for him to attack. His fury mounted like an oncoming wind and finally he shook his head, tossed his mane and rose high in the air. He came down hard, pawing the ground and lashing the wind. He squealed furiously as if to tell his foe that he, too, had led wild herds and conquered many stallions! Never had he been matched in courage and cunning! He feared no savage beast, no other stallion!

One sharp ear was turned to his own mares while the other remained pricked forward toward his foe. His fury continued to mount and again he tossed his head and rose, pawing the air. When he finally came down he seemed to be breathing fire.

Suddenly the Black moved forward. His mares followed him, smashing through the cane in their eagerness not to be left behind. But the Black had little thought for his band at this time and his speed increased with every stride. Faster and faster he ran, his action so smooth and swift, despite his bruised hoof, that it seemed as if·it would have been no trouble for him to have flown. He soared above the ground, taking longer and longer strides, his great nostrils puffed out with air. As he approached the big herd, jubilation was evident in every movement. He was ready to conquer!

Suddenly he stopped as if struck by a bullet. On the wind rang a shrill whistle, uttered not by the red leader but by still another stallion!

Among the young stallions who stood just outside the ring on guard there was one who, more than any of the others, coveted the position as supreme leader of the herd. He was milk-white in color and unlike the other young, ambitious stallions his body was un-scathed; there were no cuts, bruises or tooth marks. And yet he was a veteran of more fights than any horse in the herd with the exception of the red stallion he expected one day to dethrone. He left the ring, going downwind, his eyes like his leader's watching the strange black stallion. In the cold, bleak light of early morning, his warm nostrils could be seen reddening as he blew them out, snorting, while his great eyes bulged in their sockets. Then he again whistled his clarion call of battle and broke into a run, moving down the valley with the grace of a large white bird.

Suddenly he stopped and whirled as if undecided as to the proper method of attack. He snorted repeatedly at his black opponent, his body trembling with rage . . . or was it in sudden terror?

He reared, going up and up and up. Coming down, he looked back at the herd for the first time since he'd left it. He stood still for a moment, sniffing the air, pricking up his ears, listening to the whinnies and snorts from the mares. Then as if it had all been decided for him, he turned downwind once more.

Fire flashed in his eyes as he screamed again and again. He rose once more, lashing out with his hoofs and rocking the valley with a thunderous sound when he came down. He squealed fiercely at the Black Stallion, as if hoping to frighten him away . . . all to no avail.

Finally he bounded off on long slender legs, half on the ground, half in the air, having betrayed himself for what he was—a stallion too young, too inexperienced for the black horse who silently, quietly awaited him.

All at once the Black Stallion was no longer earthbound! He moved toward the white horse, full of life and vigor and, most of all, confidence. He had not been frightened at all by the milk-white charger who by his antics had sought to instill nameless terror within him. Often he had met such young stallions in battle, all seeking to be the chosen king of the herd and to assume leadership. They were all too eager, and this one was no different.

He watched the other coming toward him again. The milk-white stallion was running with his head bent a little too close to the ground. His pace too was irregular as if he weren't quite sure whether to lope or trot or stop.

More confident than ever, the Black Stallion prepared to meet his opponent. He knew no master, no companion save one who was not here. With marvelous flowing action he streaked across the valley floor, meeting his foe head-on!

The Black reared and lashed and whirled, his hoofs rocking the white stallion with thunderous blows. When he came down he sped around the other with the speed of summer lightning. Again he rose, coming down with battering forefeet on the other's haunches.

The white stallion sought to escape the blows, squealing in rage and pain. Flecks of foam spattered the air from his mouth. Already he knew he was defeated. His opponent's mastery of combat was far greater than his own. He could not equal the other's quickness, cunning and courage. He wheeled to get away and then, straightening out, ran across the valley, seeking the tall cane in which he might lose his pursuer. He was frightened. For here was an enemy who, he had realized from the first whirlwind charge, would cut him to pieces with slashing hoofs and teeth.

Upon reaching the cane his rush slackened, then picked up again when he discovered that the Black Stallion was close behind. For a moment it looked as though he might turn back to stand at bay and snort in defiance. But instead he kept running, now forward, now sideways, seeking to escape the black fury behind him. But there seemed to be no way of shaking him off. The white stallion was trapped.

Having humbled his enemy, the Black Stallion did not intend to kill him. He had no impulse to fling himself upon the young stallion, who was no match for him. It was one thing to kill through necessity, another to kill a beaten foe. He dropped back, letting the other seek refuge in the cane.

A few minutes later he returned to his band, favoring his bruised foot more than ever. And he screamed his high-pitched call, once more claiming this land as his very own. Yet he did not go forward to meet the red stallion, for he was too much of a veteran not to know that his quiet adversary was a most worthy one, one he dare not meet at this time. He would wait until the pain left his foot, then return. Snorting to his mares, he drove them once again through the marsh and back to the smaller valley.

Toy Land

8

The squall swept quickly from the open sea into the harbor of Chestertown, port city of the island of Antago, British West Indies. It hammered an anchored freighter a mile out in the bay and prevented stevedores from unloading further cargo into the tenders alongside. It swept on to the wharf and Custom House, then crossed the remaining seafront into the heart of the city. It washed the cobblestone streets clean before climbing the island hills and disappearing in a mist.

The sun came out again and a brilliant rainbow appeared, arching over the city and harbor. Perspiring men, naked to the waist, resumed unloading the freighter while tenders streamed back and forth to the pier. The transfer of cargo was supervised vigilantly by harbor police who wore white middies, bell-bottom trousers and flat, wide-brimmed hats while standing majestically in deep rowboats. After the heavy shower, the air was very damp and laden with the sweet, heavy odor of hundreds of bags of cane sugar stacked on the pier and waiting to be loaded onto the ship.

Within the city itself, the people of Antago emerged in throngs from banks, hotels and shops, creating a crazy tangle of noisy traffic. They overflowed the too-narrow sidewalks, spilling into the streets and scurrying along hurriedly before honking bicycles and cars. Police blew their whistles in prolonged bursts of frenzy at every intersection, seeking attention. And above all the noise a lone woman's shrill wails could be heard as she hawked the wares carried in a huge basket balanced on her head.

Behind a pink stucco wall and an iron grille gate at the end of the busy street was a quiet and stately old colonial residence. A sign on the wall read: ANTAGO POLICE AND IMMIGRATION DEPTS.

The screened doors of the building opened and a policeman accompanied by Alec Ramsay and Henry Dailey stepped onto the porch.

The police officer wore a blue uniform trimmed with gold braid. He glanced at the anchored freighter in the harbor and for a few seconds seemed to be listening to the far-off rattling of the winches and the thuds of heavy cargo being dropped into the tenders. Finally he said, with a decidedly British accent, "I'm afraid you should be leaving with your friends. We have no regular service to the States and it might be several weeks before—"

Henry interrupted. "Now that our folks know we're alive, we've got time." He nodded to Alec and added, "Plenty of it."

"I don't care how long it takes," the boy said. "I'm staying as long as there's a chance of finding my horse."

Shrugging his shoulders, the police officer said, "Even somebody as young as you shouldn't waste too much time."

A chill passed over Alec. "I might not be wasting it. We made it to land, so could he."

"We have to think he's safe," Henry told the officer. "And your commissioner has given us some hope, telling us of the lone horse seen running on your western beaches."

"It happens often that a horse breaks loose from one of the plantation corrals," the officer said patiently. "I would not set my hopes too high if I were you."

"But this one is black," Henry answered. "He could be ours."

"We'll soon find out."

"If I could just *see* him," Alec said. "You don't have to think of catching him. Just let me get one look. I'll know . . . so will he."

The officer smiled sympathetically. "It shouldn't be too difficult. Our island is small and under a high degree of cultivation. There aren't too many places for a horse to hide."

Wearing khaki trousers, cotton shirts, canvas sneakers and sun hats supplied by the city government, Alec and Henry followed the policeman into a small black sedan.   .

"We'll be back within a few hours but I'm afraid your ship will be gone by then," the officer said, starting the car.

Henry grunted. "I wish you'd stop feelin' sorry for us. We're pretty lucky just to be here at all."

"Yes, I'm sure you are."

Alec looked out the window at the avenue of green and gold coconut palms and gigantic bamboos, then at the high cane-clad hills above them. He had felt sick to his stomach for three days, ever since they'd landed on the beach south of Chestertown. His illness wasn't the result of what they'd all gone through during the crash and afterward. It was the thought of never seeing his horse again that so curled up his insides he couldn't eat or drink. He had to get over it, he told himself, otherwise he'd be no good to himself or anybody else. He had to search for the Black without panic and with confidence that it was only a question of time before finding him.

I've got to say he's alive over and over again and mean it every time. He's out there somewhere . . . if not on this island, then on another. If he was dead, I'd know it. I'd feel it every time my heart beats. I'm sure he's alive and I'm going to find him. It's just a matter of looking. If I believe that, I'm all right. . . .

To forget his horse for a moment he concentrated on the narrow, winding asphalt road before them; it scraped the doorsteps of white and cream-colored clay houses and occasionally a patchwork of frame huts. These were the homes of the workers who tilled the cane fields.

Perspiration dripped from the police officer's face onto his blue jacket. He glanced at the boy beside him, noting the serious expression on his face. "It'll be cooler up in the hills where the breeze can reach us," he said, smiling and showing very large white teeth.

Without taking his eyes off the road Alec asked, "Are there many islands in this area?" *How many would he have to search before he found the Black?*

"Well, there's a whole archipelago full if you count everything that sticks out of the water," the policeman said good-naturedly, still trying to get the boy to smile. "Our fishermen say you can't sail to the west without sighting one landfall after another."

The officer shifted to a lower gear as they climbed higher into the hills. "These islands are nothing but the tops of a long chain of submerged volcanic peaks, ringed by coral reefs. Just a bunch of toy lands strung together on a plate-glass sea, you might say."

"Are most of them inhabited?" Alec asked. *If people got a look at the Black they'd recognize him for what he was, a very valuable horse. One person would tell another and another and another. Finally the news would reach him and he and the Black would be together again.*

"Many of them are as well populated as this one,"

the policeman answered, "but there are some that are much too small and barren to support life for very long. Actually they're nothing but shoals and islets."

Alec turned away, not wanting to hear any more. He didn't want to picture his horse in such a place.

Henry asked, "Is there any boat service between the islands?"

"Freighters, if you're lucky enough to catch one going between the large islands. Then there are fishing boats and motor launches going between the smaller islands if you want to hire one. But there is no regular scheduled service if that's what you mean."

"And no planes?"

The policeman grinned broadly. "Not in this particular section of the archipelago. Our terrain is not suited for the cutting out of landing fields. Besides, most of us feel there is little need for such speedy transportation."

Stopping the car, the officer reached out through the open window to grab at a cluster of bananas hanging from a nearby tree. He handed one to Alec and one to Henry and then began peeling his own. They were high above the harbor if not many miles distant from it. Sounds carried clearly across the water and they could hear the shouting porters on the freighter and the straining noises made by the overburdened tenders.

"They have begun loading," the police officer said, pointing with his banana at the ship. "It won't be long before they leave us now." He pointed seaward where a fishing boat with sails blown out like the wings of a great bird was coming into the harbor.

"Isn't that a pretty sight?" he asked softly. "A little slow, perhaps, but beautiful . . . very beautiful and so very *quiet*."

Alec's eyes left the boat for the rainbow, which still hung faintly over the lush and fertile island. His gaze followed the arch to the point where it dipped into the distant sea. "Are there islands in that direction, too?" he asked. He was grasping at every ray of hope. Might not the rainbow be an omen, telling him where he might find his horse?

"To the northeast?" the police officer asked, following the boy's gaze. "Yes, a few, but none of any size or consequence."

They continued on and soon were climbing one line of hills after another. They passed many great plantation houses all perched high above the city and resplendent with their swimming pools and gardens. Fields of cane were everywhere and to Alec and Henry they looked like the rustling stalks of tall, straight corn to be seen in the Midwest at home. The only difference was that here towering royal palms fringed the fields and beside them flowered hedges of red, pink and yellow hibiscus.

After another hour of driving the cultivated fields dropped behind and the road wound its way through jagged upland ravines.

"This is the only section of our island too rugged to cultivate," the policeman explained.

"What's that down there?" Henry asked suddenly.

Far below there was a dark, sloping patch of land, a solid mass of jungle green surrounded by mist.

"It's an abandoned plantation," the officer explained. "Nothing more at this time of year than fields of vast mangrove swamp. During the dry season most of it is parched and baked."

Alec looked down upon the green walls of brush and jungle which seemed solid and almost impenetrable.

"Was the horse seen around here?" he asked.

"Yes, on the lower beach," the officer answered.

Sand and sea bordered one end of the abandoned fields. There the breakers of the green and blue Caribbean reached an unbroken line of jungle that edged over the bright sand.

"Who reported him?" Henry asked. "You mean someone lives in that swamp?"

"Oh yes. We have our Experimental Stock Farm Station in the old plantation house, which you can't see from here. It's a branch of our Veterinary Public Health Service," the officer explained.

"Then they were the ones who reported the horse?" Henry asked.

"Yes, after some farmers from the village just below reported seeing him on the beach." The police officer pointed to a small patch of farmland midway to the jungle. "That's the village of Crane. Let's find out if anyone has seen him since."

The village was a mere huddle of palm huts among coconut trees. It was neither clean nor picturesque and there was squalor everywhere. Donkeys, children and chickens ran about in the dirt road, while adults squatted over piles of bananas, mangoes, limes and coconuts.

The police officer brought the car to a stop before one of the huts and the men there quickly gathered around him, jabbering so excitedly Alec had difficulty making out what was being said. However, the officer seemed to understand for he quickly left the car and went along with the men. Alec and Henry followed.

A black goat lay dead behind the hut. The policeman knelt down beside it, examining a small neck wound. Finally he looked up at the group and asked, "Did he die like the cow?"

A big man nodded vigorously, perspiration streaming down his face. "We prayed hard for him to get well but he died all the same. We're being punished for some wrong we done. We're being punished for sure."

Turning back to the goat the police officer said, "Tie him to the side of my car and we'll take him to the Experimental Station. Then we'll know for sure."

He stood up, straightening his jacket casually. But his eyes disclosed his great concern. "Last week they lost a cow the same way," he stated to Alec and Henry.

"What way?" Henry asked.

"Paralytic rabies. We had her examined and found Negri bodies in the brain and spinal cord. So we're sure."

Alec and Henry said nothing. They were both well aware of the consequences of rabies. It was a disease fatal to animals and humans.

The officer went on. "We believe we know, too, how she contracted it, for there was no mistaking the bite wound."

"From a mad dog," Henry guessed, "one you've already killed?"

"No, not a dog. And I'm afraid this carrier is still very much alive and active—"

"But he must be destroyed!" Henry interrupted urgently. "He's capable of infecting human beings as well as animals!"

The police officer said gravely, patiently, "We're well aware of that, sir. The problem of our Veterinary Public Health Service is to find him. He's a winged carrier, one that unfortunately feeds on warm-blooded animals . . . *a vampire bat.*"

Alec turned to look at the villagers' palm huts which were open to all winds, and at the shelters for animals that consisted only of a roof on four poles. None offered protection from such a deadly night marauder. And the Black—assuming he was in this locality—was no better off.

Child of Darkness

9

They drove down to the beach, their eyes going often to the lifeless black goat strapped to the right fender. There was no road beyond the village they had just left and they simply used the beach, for the tide was out and the sand firm. Stiff trade winds blew in from the ocean and shell-pink clouds studded the azure sky.

They passed a small group of brightly colored boats anchored a short distance offshore. The men on board waved to the police officer; he waved back but kept going, his face grim.

"We have never before had a vampire bat on Antago," he said. "I believe he was transported from Trinidad in one of those fishing boats. The men go there frequently."

"Are you sure they have vampires in Trinidad?" Henry asked.

"Yes, and not only there. The child of darkness has long been known to be a source of annoyance and fear throughout South America . . . and in Central America and Mexico as well."

"Child of darkness?" Alec repeated. "You call him that?"

The officer shrugged his shoulders. "When I lived in Trinidad he was called that very often, especially when he chose to sleep near highly populated centers. Some people took him as much for granted as a domesticated animal or"—he turned to the sea before finishing—"perhaps a rat is a better comparison."

"Yet they knew he could carry disease?" Alec asked incredulously.

"So can rats," the policeman answered quietly.

"But the vampire lives on the blood of his victims."

"So does a horsefly, a mosquito or a tick."

"You sound almost resigned," Henry said grimly.

"Not at all, just realistic. You asked, you know, and I'm only doing my best to acquaint you with the facts which are well known to public health authorities in all tropical countries. You, of course, do not have such a problem in your temperate climate where the vampire bat does not exist."

"Thanks for that," Henry said.

"He ranges from southern Brazil to southern Mexico. But until now I had never heard of any in the West Indies."

Alec interrupted. "I'm certain I saw bats flying outside last night, lots of them."

"We have many other species, of course, but they are harmless, eating only fruit and insects. There's one species, too, that I've seen fishing with the pelicans and terns."

"Then the vampire bat is the black sheep of the tribe," Henry said thoughtfully.

"I suppose you can call him that," the police officer said, nodding his big head. "There's no doubt that he will attack any animals loose in fields or tethered in open stalls. He'll go after fowl asleep in roosts, too."

"And humans?" Alec asked.

"Only when he can't get the food he needs from animals and poultry," the officer answered gravely.

Henry's eyes swept the steaming jungle close to the beach road. "And since he must bite in order to feed, it's easy for him to transmit disease . . . in this case one of the deadliest of all, rabies."

The policeman nodded. "Don't forget, too, that's probably the way he became infected, by biting diseased livestock in Trinidad."

Alec shifted uneasily in his seat. He said, "And by means of flight it's easy for him to spread infection."

Again the policeman nodded. "I've seen them winging their way across the open sea between Trinidad and the South American mainland, a distance of twelve miles. But usually unless there's a mass migration they stay close to their sleeping places, located mostly in mountains and forests. However, like rats they are apt to be transported through sloops and other vessels plying between the islands. It's a wonder we haven't had this problem before."

"Why do you think there's only *one* vampire bat here? Couldn't there be many more?" Alec asked.

"Probably, but I doubt it. There have been so few victims, only the cow and now this goat. . . ."

"No people? You're sure?" Alec asked, remembering the open huts.

"Examination of the villagers has disclosed no characteristic bites of the vampire."

Alec cast another glance at the dense green jungle, thinking of all the horrible stories he'd read about the vampire bat. "Is he a very big bat?" he asked.

"No, he's not. His wingspread usually isn't more than a foot and he has a very short body like a mouse. In fact he looks very much like a mouse with wings, being gray or reddish-brown in color. Yet in flight he's as agile and graceful as a swallow."

Alec shuddered at the comparison. "Is it true they use their wings to fan a victim to sleep before biting him so nothing will be felt?"

"No, that's purely an imaginative story."

"Just his being a bloodsucker is bad enough for me," Henry said grimly.

"He does not suck blood," the policeman corrected. "He simply makes a small, oval-shaped, superficial wound and laps the blood that wells."

"You're quite an authority on him," Henry said almost disgustedly.

"Perhaps, for we have to accept such problems here in the tropics. Our veterinary surgeon knows more about the matter than anyone else. It's his responsibility to catch the vampire and check the spread of the disease."

"Is he the man we're going to see?" Alec asked, glancing at the dead goat.

"Yes, he'll be at the Station if he's not out hunting the vampire. Of course he's well acquainted with the jungle roosts of the bats."

Henry shuddered. "I can think of pleasanter jobs."

The policeman smiled sympathetically. "I'm afraid you're prejudiced against *all* bats," he said, "and you shouldn't be."

"I'll admit that what you've told me about them hasn't helped."

"Did you know that bats were flying millions of years before our own race appeared on earth?"

Henry shook his head.

"And that no other mammal has ever attained the power of flight?"

"No, I didn't," Henry answered.

"Bats entered the realm of the air some fifty million years ago by changing their forefeet into wings, lengthening their fingers and spreading a wide skin between them."

"Yet they're creatures of the night," Henry said thoughtfully. "I wonder why?"

"Perhaps because they have fewer enemies and competitors at night," the officer said. "No one really knows very much about them. Since earliest times they've aroused the imagination of men, yet they're still something of a mystery."

"Maybe that's because of the way they behave," Henry said, trying to smile. "Here they are, creatures that fly like birds, bite like beasts, hide by day and attack in the dark."

"Perhaps," agreed the officer, smiling. "But don't forget too that their faces and prominent ears bear a remarkable likeness to human beings."

"If you say so," Henry said. "I wouldn't know myself. I don't even care to find out."

The Experimental Station was just a little way in from the beach. It looked cool and spacious, occupying a large court and consisting of a main building, a dozen stables, several stock pens and some cages. Leaving the car, Alec and his companions went into the building and entered a laboratory. It was hardly more than a large living room, bare of furniture except for a couple of small tables, marble-topped and unadorned, a few straight chairs and an old rocking chair.

There were empty cages everywhere as well as collecting bags, cans and tins. It was obvious that whatever else was to be found at the government station this room was the headquarters of the small man seated at one of the tables. He brought a microscope into focus, then glanced up at his visitors.

"Good morning, Doctor," the police officer said briskly. He introduced Alec and Henry, then added very solemnly, "I have a goat from the village that died the same way as the cow. He carries the bite of the vampire."

The veterinarian put his microscope away. "I am not surprised," he said gravely. "But the vampire will infect no others. I've found out where he sleeps."

"Where?"

"I saw him come out of the big cave with the other bats. I'll get him today."

Alec said, "A horse was also reported in this area. Have you seen him, Doctor?"

The veterinarian looked up, his round face puzzled. "A horse?"

"Yes."

"Oh, I remember," he said kindly. "The villagers reported seeing one on the beach."

"But you've found no trace . . . ?"

"Trace?"

"Tracks, I mean," Alec explained. "Hoofprints, during your search for the vampire."

"You see, he may be *our* horse," Henry interjected.

"Yes, I did see some tracks," the veterinarian answered thoughtfully. "They were in front of Bat Cave, the place I mentioned a moment ago."

"Where the vampire lives?" Henry asked.

The veterinarian nodded. "In fact the horse might even be using that same cave for shelter. It would be easy enough to find out. If his tracks are inside . . ."

Henry shuddered. "He might already have been bitten by the bat and infected."

"Very true," the veterinarian replied soberly. He stood up. "I was about to leave for the cave. If you care to come along . . ." He stopped, his eyes turning to the police officer.

"It's up to them," the officer said. "Hunting vampires isn't to everyone's liking."

"We're looking for a horse, not a bat," Henry said. "But since the trail leads to the same place . . ." He paused, turning to Alec. "Is that the way you feel about it, too?"

Alec nodded.

The veterinarian shrugged his thin shoulders and began gathering his materials together. "You won't have to enter the cave unless you think it necessary."

"Aren't you afraid of being attacked yourself?" Henry asked.

"No, he'll leave me alone unless he's cornered."

"But isn't that what you intend to do?" Henry asked.

"It's true that I hope to capture him alive for use in my experimental work." Making his way around the table, the veterinarian added, "In the tropics one even gets used to coping with vampires. Why, some islanders regard him as a guardian spirit and believe that to kill him will cause one to fall ill."

A chill swept over Alec. "But his food is blood," he said in a horrified voice.

"As natural to him as milk or coffee is to us, so who are we to judge?" the veterinarian asked patiently. "And the loss of the victim's blood isn't serious unless prolonged. Only when the vampire is infected with a disease such as rabies do we have a very grave problem."

"Then you'd better shoot if you get near him," Henry said.

"If necessary," the veterinarian replied quietly.

As they left the big room Alec shuddered at the thought that the horse living near Bat Cave might turn out to be the Black.

Bat Cave

10

It was the middle of the morning when the small group entered the jungle, the veterinarian carrying a long-handled net and machete. All four hikers wore leather boots and gloves, and they walked in single file through a green maze of dangling lianas as thick as a man's arm.

The veterinarian led the way, using twisted roots for footholds and seldom looking back. Alec was behind him, even when they went splashing through a fast-flowing stream of jade-colored water. He jumped the water plants and hurried around a dark labyrinth of mangrove roots and giant fronds before entering the dark green wall of jungle again. Sandflies nipped his face and he brushed them off angrily. The jungle was broiling with heat and insects.

At a small clearing in a coconut grove the veterinarian stopped the party for a rest.

Henry sat down tiredly and said, "No horse came this way."

"No, he used the beach," the veterinarian replied. "This is shorter if not as easy." He opened a coconut with a blow of his machete and handed it to Henry. "Here, this will make you feel better," he said, smiling.

Henry drank some of the liquid and passed the coconut on to Alec. "Does the vampire sleep only in caves?" he asked the veterinarian.

"No, he'll use rooftops, hollow trees and drains if necessary."

"Are there many bats in the cave we're going to?" Alec asked.

"Perhaps a hundred of various species," the veterinarian replied.

"How can you be sure the vampire returned to this one?" Henry asked.

"He prefers living in large communities and his homing instinct is very strong. He'll be there, all right."

Alec stood up. "You say there's never been a vampire on Antago before to your knowledge. What makes you so sure?"

The police officer answered for the veterinarian. "The bite of the vampire is not easily mistaken. Sooner or later we would have found it on some of our livestock.

"I worked in Trinidad during one of its worst outbreaks of bat rabies," the officer went on. "We had a trained squad for the destruction of bats alone. We used to travel like this looking for their sleeping places during the daytime. It was our most effective way of control. We used nets, poison dust, clubs and cages when we found them."

"What time do they usually leave their caves?" Alec asked.

"About dusk, and on into the night," the veterinarian answered, rising to his feet.

"The expression 'blind as a bat' must fall short of the truth if they live in caves and hunt at night," Henry said thoughtfully.

"That's so," the veterinarian said. "Actually their eyes, although small, are very well developed."

"You mean they can *see* in the dark?" Alec asked.

"Not exactly, but they can get around as well as if they *could* see. They have an acute sense of hearing and sensitive nerve endings in the wings. While flying they emit shrill, high-pitched cries which serve to guide their flight by means of reflected sound waves."

"Don't they fly during the day?" Henry asked.

"Only when disturbed or sick. Strangely enough they don't seem to be dazzled by the sun and they fly very accurately."

"Don't they have any natural enemies that might kill them?" Alec asked.

"A few," the veterinarian answered. "Some owls, hawks and snakes eat them, but usually fighting among themselves accounts for more deaths than anything else."

"If this rabid vampire bat fights . . ." Henry began.

The veterinarian nodded. "He'll infect harmless species with rabies and then we really will have trouble controlling the disease. Now let's proceed."

He led the way through another tangled green trail that was ankle-deep in mud and, when necessary, cut his way through the vine barricades with his machete. Half-bent in an effort to keep their balance in the slimy footing, the others followed him. Finally they began a steep climb and within a half-hour found themselves on a slight plateau.

"Here we are," the veterinarian said quietly.

Alec, looking about for some sign of the horse, spied a large black opening on a hillside opposite the one on which they were standing. "Is that Bat Cave?" he asked.

Following Alec's gaze, the veterinarian nodded.

They moved forward, Alec fearful of what he might find there. Finally they stood before the huge black opening, their eyes searching the soft earth.

Any hoofprints that had been in front of the cave had been washed away by the heavy rains. But just within the entrance they found them, large and oval-shaped on a floor that was covered with the black, tarry droppings of the bats.

"They're not the Black's," Alec said, and there was no disappointment in his voice or eyes.

"No," Henry agreed, "they're too small." He, too,

was relieved. He wanted to find the Black anywhere but here!

The veterinarian had stepped farther into the cave, his flashlight probing the darkness. Then he held it steady, and within its glare they all saw the still, dead body of the horse on the floor. He was the color of the night but there his resemblance to the Black ended, for he was small and wiry.

They kneeled beside him, the veterinarian pointing out the shallow, clean-cut scoop on the horse's withers. "The mark of the vampire," he said. "It was not an easy death for him."

Alec turned away from the rigid body, his eyes filled with tears.

The police officer said, "Don't feel sorry for him. He's better off now."

"Yes," the veterinarian agreed, rising to his feet, "the worst is long over."

Henry peered into the cave's blackness. "Give me a club and I'll go with you," he said evenly.

"If you're serious, you could help me more by using your flashlight," the veterinarian answered.

"Not unless you promise me you'll use your gun instead of the net," Henry said, eying the revolver in the man's waist holster.

"I'll go," Alec interrupted, removing his own flashlight from his belt clip.

Henry turned to him. "Okay," he said quietly. "I was going anyway."

Nodding to the police officer, the veterinarian said,

"Let's be on our way then. All I ask is that you hold
the light on the vampire once we find him. I'll do the
rest. I'll take all the chances."

"I hope so," Henry said resignedly.

They walked toward the back of the cave until they
reached a broad minelike shaft with an improvised
ladder. The veterinarian climbed down, followed
closely by Henry and Alec, with the police officer last.
The floor of the tunnel at the bottom consisted of red
mud and Alec's feet almost slid from beneath him as
he stepped down from the last rung of the ladder.

As they went along, the tunnel widened and water
could be seen seeping from the walls and from the
crevices in the floor. It made the mud deeper and the
going harder. Alec heard Henry panting as he tried to
keep up with the veterinarian.

The air became hot and heavy and there was a
sweetish odor to it. In the light from his flash Alec saw
a seething mass of centipedes and spiders on the walls,
while roaches and other bugs rubbed against each
other on the ceiling. His gaze quickly returned to
Henry's back and the ankle-deep mud of the tunnel
floor.

But there was no shutting his eyes to the creatures
that lived within this dark world. Soon they entered a
big chamber with an arched ceiling that rose all of fifty
feet above them. There Alec saw clusters of bats of
different sizes and species swarming on the rough and
jagged stone. Some were as small as mice while others
were as big as rabbits. All hung by their legs with

heads bent against their chests and partly covered by voluminous wings.

The bats did not move in the glare of the lights as the veterinarian's searching gaze swept over them.

"He doesn't seem to be here," he said finally. "We'll try the next chamber."

"How'll we know him?" Henry asked.

"You won't have any trouble. He has a peculiar gait of his own. You'll see him run along the walls and try to hide."

"I don't especially want to see him," Henry answered grimly. "I just want you to *kill* him."

They sloshed their way through the subterranean sea of mud into the next chamber. It was longer and wider than the first one but not more than eight feet high.

"We can reach him here," the veterinarian said, extending his net toward the ceiling.

The flashlights disclosed hundreds more bats, all hanging in bunched masses so close together it seemed they would smother. And all were of medium size.

"Fruit eaters," the veterinarian said disappointedly, his eyes following the beams of the lights. But suddenly he shifted his own flashlight to a far corner of the chamber.

The wall on that side was gray and green with age and fungus. Across it, with a sudden scurrying of feet, ran a bat! He raced with the speed of a rat and darted into a large crevice.

The veterinarian gasped. "That's the one!" he whispered excitedly. "Put out all your lights for a minute."

They turned off their flashlights until the veterinarian told them to turn them on again. There was no sign of the vampire. He was still inside the crevice.

"Turn off your lights again and maybe he'll come out," the veterinarian ordered.

Once more they were in complete darkness and Alec felt the mud oozing above his ankles. The veterinarian was at home here but he wasn't. The chamber was very hot and oppressive, and what made it worse was the powerful and unpleasant smell of the bats. He heard squeaks in the darkness, some near, some far away. Was the vampire himself close by? Alec almost turned on his light to find out.

The flitting of shadowy wings bothered him more than anything else. Suddenly a bat flew past his ears with a swish and a second later he heard Henry snort in alarm. Then in further panic the old trainer switched on his light. In its beam Alec noticed at once that the bats were no longer hanging in clusters or asleep. Their heads were up and they seemed to be ready to let go of the rock and fly away at any moment.

"Leave on your light but don't jiggle it," the veterinarian told Henry irritably. "Anything we do now will only stir them up more."

But suddenly one of the bats dropped on Henry's head and the older man let out a great shout. His roar, echoing and re-echoing through the chambers, caused the bats to start flying and suddenly the chamber was filled with streaming forms.

The men threw up gloved hands in front of their faces to ward off the flying bodies. Louder than Henry's shout were the guttural squeaks of the bats and the roaring beat of their wings. The noise was deafening.

Finally, when it became quiet again, the veterinarian said, "I'm afraid the vampire left with the others, but keep your lights on the crevice to make sure."

"I'm sorry," Henry apologized, "but that—"

"You couldn't help it," the veterinarian said. "There's no need to apologize. And after all he might still be here. Watch now. If he comes out, he'll scramble sideways first, much like a crab."

They waited in silence, the dead, stagnant air inducing a clammy sweat which was most uncomfortable. Alec was conscious of the living wall beside him, for he could hear the workings of hundreds of insects. He told himself that even the cool breeze of bats' wings might be easier to endure than this.

Suddenly the vampire came out of the crevice, crawling along the wall a few steps at a time. He seemed to be completely ignorant of their presence yet he was in the full glare of their lights. He had raised himself high on his hind legs while his long thumbs were directed forward and outward, supporting the fore end of his body and serving as feet.

Raising his net, the veterinarian waited for him to come a little closer. "Notice the way he walks," he whispered. "All other species flop along the ground in the most awkward, ungainly way, but he—"

The veterinarian stopped talking for the vampire had paused as if suddenly undecided about the light. He seemed more disturbed than afraid. He wrinkled his ugly little face and bared his razorlike teeth in what appeared to be a sneer. A musty, acrid odor which became almost overpowering emanated from him.

Henry shivered. "Go ahead, catch him if you're going to," he whispered uneasily. "Or use your gun."

"Don't flicker your light so," came the sharp reprimand from the veterinarian. "I can't reach him yet."

The vampire looked around and squeaked faintly. At the same time his eyes became more bright and shining. He took another step, then another, moving closer and closer to the men.

Suddenly the veterinarian made his move. He swung the net quickly with the skill of a man who has caught many thousands of bats and insects. But fast as he was, the vampire was faster. There was only a flash of wings as the bat left the wall too quickly for the eye to follow him.

"Shoot him!" Henry shouted, his words deadened by swishing wings. But the vampire was gone.

For a moment they stood in dejected silence, then the veterinarian said, "He's left the cave to find another place to sleep for the day. He'll be back with the others tomorrow morning. I'll get him then."

"Where do you think he's gone?" Alec asked.

"Almost any place nearby—a tree, a bush, a drain, anything that provides cover from the sun."

"With no chance of finding him?" Alec prodded.

"Very unlikely. It's best to wait until he returns here." The man turned to Henry, his face pale. "I'll use the gun tomorrow. We can't take any more chances."

"Good," Henry said. "Fine. I just hope you're not too late."

It was a little after noon when they left the Experimental Station and drove down the beach again.

"It's too bad you missed your boat for this," the police officer said.

"We've got lots more searching to do," Henry said. "What's the nearest island?"

"Inhabited?"

"It doesn't matter," Alec interjected.

"There's one out there, twenty miles away. Not much to it, though," The police officer pointed to the northeast and Alec recalled the early morning rainbow that had arched in the same direction.

"Could it support life?" Henry asked.

"For a horse?"

"Sure," Henry said irritably. "That's what we're looking for, isn't it?"

"It has a short spit where wild grass grows and there's fresh water. The rest of it is nothing but rock, solid rock."

"What's its name?" Alec asked.

"Azul—that's Spanish for blue. How it got that name, I wouldn't know. Nothing blue about it at all."

Alec turned to Henry. "I have a strange feeling about that island, Henry. With a good boat we could make it there and back before dark."

The old trainer glanced at the fishing vessels anchored just offshore and nodded. "He could be there as well as anywhere else," he agreed. Then, turning to the police officer, he asked, "Could you recommend any one of these boats for hire?"

"Try the *Night Owl*," the officer answered, pointing to a black-painted motor launch. "She's the sturdiest and her skipper knows these waters better than anyone else."

Alec liked everything about the vessel but her name. It didn't appeal to him just then because he associated the night with the marauding vampire. But on the other hand the name *Night Owl* might be a good omen, for hadn't the veterinarian said that the owl was one of the few natural enemies of the bat?

Henry said, "Let's hire her, Alec. We've got nothing to lose."

Alec nodded assent, completely unaware that he had everything in the world to lose, including his very life. For in the cabin of the *Night Owl* slept the vampire, having chosen that vessel in which to spend the rest of the day. The bat hung by his hind feet with his sharp claws and head down, partly covered by a wing. He slept comfortably, awaiting the coming of night when he would set out once more to feed on another's blood.

Herd Stallion

11

The Black Stallion had waited three days for the dull pain to leave his foot and was fast becoming impatient with his handicap. The late-afternoon sun shone upon his sweaty body. He was hot and yet he would not leave his station, guarding his band with all the alertness of the hunted. His large eyes were as keen as those of the eagle as he watched his young mares, knowing that never before had they enjoyed such freedom. His nostrils were dilated and occasionally he tossed his heavily maned neck and uttered a high, bugling snort. Oh, but *he* had known such freedom as this! He loved the blowing of the wind and the green grass; there was nothing to equal the pride and joy of the wild ones!

Yet everything this horse was stemmed from his

forebears' close association with man. The desert
Bedouin had bred endurance, speed and intelligence
into his ancestors, creating them for desert warfare.
For generation after generation, in constant search of
the perfect horse they had followed the practice of
breeding only superior animals. The Black could have
been their ultimate goal, for there was nothing lacking
in his conformation, speed, intelligence and courage.

This land was new to him and yet he knew the grass
was rich in nourishment and that there was something
in the very air on which a horse thrived. But true to
his desert heritage he denied himself the luxurious,
tempting grass for he did not want to become too
content or lazy. He had many things to do and could
do them best if he was a little hungry and thirsty.

It was easy to see that many other horses had grazed
in this valley. Their hoofprints were everywhere and
they were especially heavy near the stream that cut
the floor of the small valley. He again looked fondly at
his mares and fillies, some of them drinking, others
grazing and pawing the grass. They were not wild but
settled in their ways. Free as they were now, they
looked even more beautiful and spirited to him than
they had in their stalls. Their coats were dark brown,
the color he liked best of all.

They were not only spirited but content, nickering
to each other and occasionally standing sociably
alongside each other, head to tail, switching flies and
insects from each other's face.

He turned again to the hoofprints left by the other

horses, well-worn trails with heaps of manure every-where. He found and smelled another stallion's mounds, and his blood coursed through him faster. Nervously he got down and rolled in some loose earth, then quickly got up and went to the stream. But instead of drinking he sloshed around in the stream, muddying it.

He raised his head almost immediately, looking again at his mares, for he must guard them against all other stallions. The faintest signal from him could send them into the water or racing over the ground. Again he smelled the manure of the other stallion. Then he looked around but found nothing to arouse his suspicions.

He selected the highest ground near his band and grazed a little, eating in short, fast bites. Then he took a few sips of water from the stream, his ears working as he drank. He did no more than refresh himself, lifting his head and letting big drops fall back into the stream. He must not be loaded down with water. It would only stiffen his muscles and shorten his wind.

He moved around his small band, stopping occa-sionally to grab a mouthful of choice grass. His glistening black body shone majestically in the late afternoon sun. He was the picture of awesome fierceness, ready to do battle at the slightest provoca-tion. Again he came to a stop, this time to sniff the wind. His sensitive nostrils picked up a faint whiff of a scent that caused his blood to start racing through his body.

He stepped a little faster about his band, his muscles moving with the smooth power of coiled springs. He looked as he did when going to the post, his flint-hard hoofs beating rhythmically; all that was missing was Alec Ramsay astride his back. Suddenly he broke into a lope, his tail which had been almost touching the ground now swirling high behind him. His long foretop too streamed back, getting in his eyes; irritated, he tossed his head, flinging the hair farther back so he might see his mares. He snorted to attract their attention, hoping they would notice what tremendous vitality he had.

He swept around the band several times, keeping close to the stream where the soft ground was easier on his bruised foot. He didn't want to limp before the mares or show any sign of weakness. He cleared his nostrils, snorting repeatedly. He wanted the mares to feel as wild as he did, and he knew it would take very little coaxing. By nature they were lovers of freedom just as he was . . . except that they had never known the delights of living wild and free. But perhaps they had dreamed of it and now it was theirs as well as *his!* Never again would they have to live a life of domesticity! Once more he stopped to throw back his head and sniff the wind. He didn't look for another stallion, for his nostrils sought to catch a more familiar scent. Finally he bent down to crop the grass, grazing in alertness, never quite sure, never quite still.

Soon he would steal the other leader's mares. He knew it would not be easy, for his opponent was as cunning and strong as he. It would be a furious fight, ending in the death of one of them. Neither would be driven away. Each would stand his ground until the very end. Each coveted all the mares or none.

He watched his mares and fillies grazing peacefully; they were content in the knowledge that he would protect them. He wandered a short distance away from them. At once they stopped eating as if apprehensive, and no longer did they whisk flies from each other but laid back their ears and kicked out. They moved with him, not wanting to be left alone.

The Black Stallion stopped, standing more rigid than ever, his nostrils dilated. The wind from the sea to the south blew strong, and although the scent was still some miles away he knew it well. No longer did he need to search the moving air for faint clues. He was certain of the news it carried.

He stood towering above his harem, lord of all he surveyed and wild with freedom! Yet in his joy he became uneasy, and the silence and solitude of the valley were broken by the working of his nostrils as he continued to sniff upwind. He gave no warning to his mares but uttered bugle snorts of which he alone knew the meaning.

Finally the Black moved. He ran around the mares fretfully, stopping more than once to sniff the breeze. Then he scanned the distant rock as if looking for something, and bolted again.

Upon reaching high ground, he stopped once more to survey his band. He inhaled the air deeply and exhaled it without snorting or whinnying. One of the mares started toward him and he drove her back. Trotting again, he circled the small valley as if undecided upon his next move. When the band tried to follow him he wheeled on the mares, squealing and biting to send them back.

Finally, as if he'd made up his mind what to do, he dashed around the mares and whipped them all into a run, driving them down the dry-stream gorge leading to the big valley and the home of the red stallion!

He led them through the marsh and onto the sea of blue grass. Quickly he found the large herd of horses grazing midway down the valley. He coveted the beautiful mares, and he took the time to let his eyes run fondly over them, the dark bays and chestnuts, the grays and an occasional white-and-black one. Many of them bore the scars of battle. Like stallions, the mares fought constantly, whether in a contest of strength or in anger or because of jealousy.

Most of the mares had stopped grazing at the sight of him but they did not flee or appear to be frightened. Yet they were alert to the signals being given them by the young stallions who stood apart from the herd acting as sentinels. They stood with their heads high, proud and free.

The Black's own mares were far more excitable and undecided. They circled him constantly as if afraid the wild herd would charge them. At the same time there was a strong tendency on their part to wheel, dart away from him and join the large mass of horses.

Suddenly the wild ones moved in unison, running to higher ground, and the earth shook to the sound of their plunging hoofs. The Black's mares became more uneasy than ever and only his sharp commands kept them from stampeding toward the wild runners. He knew they felt the strong urge of herd instinct despite the domesticity they had always known. They tossed their heads and manes, eager to run with the others. The Black snorted at them, refusing to set them free. And during all this time he didn't take his eyes from the lone chestnut stallion who stood apart from the herd. There was the king!

Some of the Black's mares sought to join the wild herd but he ran them down quickly, kicking and biting their shoulders. He kept them in a tightly packed bunch, jealous of their interest in the other stallions, and so fierce was he that they abandoned their attempts to escape.

Raising his head high, the Black turned to gaze again at his opponent. The red one stood clear of his herd, letting the others form their own groups, but there was no doubt that he was dominating them and keeping them together. His signals to the rank and file consisted of slight sounds and movements. The younger stallions watched him and waited, completely submissive to his bidding. Occasionally he had them race around the herd and bring order to the mares and colts by nipping them with their teeth. They squealed loudly while driving laggard colts into position, ramming into them at full speed and kicking. Finally the great herd was huddled together, becoming part of the colorful valley, splashing it with varied colors— blacks, bays and grays, roans, duns and pure whites.

The red stallion continued to stand quietly, looking down the valley at his black opponent. The antics of his mares and young stallions hadn't pressed him into action. He was the picture of alertness and vitality.

The Black sniffed the strong wind from the south, then moved swiftly about his small band on hoofs that barely touched the ground. He shook his head, still undecided. He swept about his band again, then shrieked his challenge of combat. But he didn't go forth to meet the herd stallion. Instead he breathed in the upwind with a sharp whistling sound, his head held higher than ever. Suddenly he whirled and hurled himself at his own huddled mares, scattering them! Furiously he drove them down the valley toward the big herd, their racing hoofs sending clods of sod flying into the air.

He followed them, driving them on faster and faster by squealing and biting. He appeared ready for a vicious onslaught and a bloody fight with the red stallion! His ears were flat against his head and his teeth were bared, ready to ravage. He made the mares run as fast as they could go and their plunging hoofs echoed in the valley. Quickly they neared the big herd. The Black whistled again, his eyes blazing.

The young, wild stallions came forward to meet the band of mares, coveting them. The Black drove his band on, still going at full speed. Just before reaching the herd he scattered his mares and the young stallions followed. The Black's blazing eyes swept to the red stallion, and suddenly he saw him, too, make his move for the new mares.

It was then that the Black Stallion uttered his loudest whistle yet. But it was not one of challenge! Instead he wheeled away from his mares, his nostrils filled with a scent carried from beyond the herd. Galloping, he swept past the others, his hoofs speeding over the ground like a bird in full flight!

He never looked back to see the young stallions take *his* mares into the herd. Nor did his large bright eyes seek the red leader. It was enough that he was unmolested and running upwind!

He swept into the tall cane, bending the stalks before him. Just beyond was a dark narrow cleavage in the southern wall of the valley and it was toward this that he streaked, slowing only when he had entered it. For a hundred yards the high walls rose on either side of him and then widened forming a canyon. The ground was soft and free of rock.

The Black went forward at a trot, breathing the air deeply, and his excitement mounted. He neighed shrilly once, then again. He ran as far as he could go and then stood still, the yellow walls of the canyon rising high above him. He shrilled his cries over and over again until the canyon reverberated with his great longing for the boy he loved.

Island Fortress

12

The *Night Owl* lay just off the southern spit of Azul Island and the tall, heavy black man at the wheel said, "We can go ashore if you like, boss, but you can see 'bout everything from here."

Alec and Henry stood at his side, their eyes searching the spit for some sign of the Black. As the fisherman had said, there wasn't too much to be seen of Azul Island—nothing but the sandy spit and yellow rock—or so it appeared from the sea.

Alec's gaze wandered over the wind-swept spit, finally resting on the towering stone that climbed into the sky forming a dome that gleamed in the last rays of the setting sun.

"That's a lot of rock," he said, more to himself than to anyone else.

The fisherman heard Alec. "Over nine miles of it," he said, pulling down his big straw hat and shielding his eyes from the sun, "and good for nothing."

Henry pointed to the narrow wooden pier extending into the water from the spit. "But why the pier if there's nothing to the island but solid rock?"

"Just for emergency landings. There was a time, too, when we had some horses here."

"Horses?" Alec asked eagerly.

The fisherman grinned, disclosing large square teeth. "Well, if you can call them that," he said apologetically. "Pretty small and scrawny they were, living wild like they did on that hunk of sand. 'Course it's a wonder they survived at all."

Henry's eyes swept over the barren spit. "But what did they graze on?"

"Oh, there's grass there, most of it growing up near where the rocks begin. It's sparse all right but hardy. Horses could live on it because it absorbs every bit of moisture in the ground."

"And there must be fresh water holes," Alec said, his gaze taking in the sand dunes.

"A few of them, poor but enough to keep the beasts alive."

"But why were the horses left here at all?" Alec asked.

"It was sort of a government project," the fisherman explained. "Or at least the government protected the horses for a while."

"What was the story?" Henry asked, keenly interested.

The boat rolled softly on the swells. "It goes back centuries, to 1669 to be exact," the fisherman began. "They say—that's the local newspaper—that at that time our island of Antago was taken over by the Spaniards."

"You mean the Conquistadores," Alec asked, "men like Cortés, Pizarro and Balboa?"

"I suppose so," the fisherman said, his eyes on the sea, "if that was their names. Anyway, they used Antago, since it wasn't too far off the South American mainland, as a supply base. They put together their armies there before setting out to fight the Incas and Aztecs."

"And to plunder them of their gold," Henry mused.

"But what's that got to do with this island and the horses?" Alec asked impatiently.

"Well, there came a time when the Spaniards had to run for it themselves," the fisherman explained. "The British and French pirates got too strong for them and started sacking Antago. The Spaniards spread out to other islands 'round here, trying to get back safely to their homeland. One of the places they landed was supposed to be this Azul. At least, the papers say the horses that were found here later were direct descendants of those the Conquistadores rode."

The fisherman's eyes roved over the barren land. "I don't believe it because I don't think anyone in his right mind would have come to this rock in the first place," he concluded abruptly. "Even the Spaniards. Anyway, the government took off the last of the horses a year ago."

Alec sat down, the swells making him a little queasy. For a moment more his gaze remained on this island of stone that thrust itself up out of the sea. Blue waters churned white going over submerged coral before crashing against the precipitous walls. The heavy thudding of the waves seemed ominous, the sound rising above that made by the boat's throbbing engines. Azul Island made Alec think of a huge castle or fortress out of the Middle Ages, its cliffs seeming to say to all who would enter, "Turn back!"

Finally he said, "I wonder if there is more to this island than just the sandspit."

"There isn't," the fisherman said quietly. "I've been in these waters long enough to know. It's rock, nothing but a big boulder plunked into the sea."

Henry watched the fisherman steady the vessel, keeping it well away from the submerged coral; then he squinted into the sun. "But did you ever get close enough to find out for sure?" he asked.

Carefully, expertly, the man turned the wheel, guiding the boat between two coral reefs. His eyes never left the shadowy waters before him. There was no doubt that he knew this particular area very well.

"I've been as close as anybody, I guess," he said quietly.

"And you saw no breaks in the wall that could be used as an entrance of some sort?" Henry asked.

The fisherman grinned while shifting his ponderous weight in his seat. "Nothing but sheer rock," he repeated, "and if you have the luck to get close enough to look at it you might be unlucky enough to have the sea smash you to pieces against it. No, boss, I have cast my nets in these waters many times and I know it is best to stay clear of this island. It is only for the devil and his disciples," he concluded, his eyes sweeping skyward.

Alec looked above, too. All he could see was a large black bird soaring above the dome of Azul Island. "Are there other islands nearby?" he asked finally.

"Several." The fisherman studied Alec. "We can go to them but it will mean spending the night here rather than returning to Antago."

Alec looked at Henry questioningly.

"It will cost only a little more than if we return to Antago," the fisherman went on. He ran his tongue along his lower lip. "It will soon be dark."

"I *would* like to look around here a little more," Alec admitted.

"So would I," Henry said thoughtfully. "The story's interesting even if it isn't true."

Thinking of the extra money he would earn, the fisherman smiled and said warmly, "We can put in now, then."

"No," Henry said, "run a little more along the cliffs. We have time, and there may be something to see."

"Are there binoculars on board?" Alec asked.

"Below on the lower bunk," the fisherman answered. "But you will see no more of this island with them than with the naked eye."

"Perhaps not," Alec admitted, going through the

companionway. Below deck he rubbed his stomach gently. It was upset, due either to the day's excitement or to the rolling of the vessel. He picked up the binoculars but instead of returning to the deck stretched out on the lower bunk and closed his eyes. *Just for a moment*, he thought. *Only a moment*.

He didn't know how many minutes he'd been there when a faint stirring in the far corner of the cabin caused him to open his eyes. The boat was rolling gently on the swells and the light coming through the porthole was almost gone. Sleepy, he closed his eyes again only to snap them open a moment later. Was he awake or dreaming? The air was hot and oppressive. Had he actually heard the slight, familiar squeak of a bat or was his imagination playing tricks on him?

He stared into the darkened corner, looking for shadowy wings. Was there a blacker than black object hanging there or was he recalling too vividly his experiences in Bat Cave?

As his vision became more adjusted to the dim light he had no doubt as to what was there. *The vampire bat hung by one leg, his head bent against his chest and partly covered by a softly moving wing.*

Alec fought to keep from yelling at the top of his lungs. There was only one thing to do—kill the bat before it awakened. It had to be done quickly, quietly, *now*.

There was a broom beside his bunk. Not much of a weapon but it would have to do. The vampire was stirring still more. If he swung hard, he might at least stun it and then get help from the men above. He recalled the veterinarian's warnings—vampires would bite viciously when caught or provoked—and he wished he had on the heavy leather gloves loaned him earlier by the veterinarian.

Alec lay motionless, his hand tightening about the broomstick. He told himself that he wasn't going to be the vampire's next victim, but his hands and body were clammy with fear. Turning over cautiously on his side, he put one foot on the floor, then the other. Quietly he rose to a sitting position and then got to his feet. Softly he moved forward, one slow step at a time.

He was almost within reach of the vampire when there was a quick movement of its wings and suddenly small bright eyes were staring into his. The vampire continued hanging downward but now his lips were drawn back, disclosing long, sharp-edged teeth. And from the tiny mouth came a low, rumbling snarl.

Alec was afraid to make the first move so he remained stock-still, staring back at the vampire. The bat seemed disinclined to move also but began uttering soft, hissing cries. Alec wondered if the squeals could be heard on deck and if the men would come to his aid. Or was it better for him to strike now while he still had a chance? Perhaps if he swung hard and fast he might just be able to reach the vampire.

Alec made up his mind and swung the broomstick with all his might. The vampire let go of his perch, flying directly at Alec with mouth wide open. The broomstick struck him a glancing blow and he fell to the cabin floor. But he did not lie there stunned. Instead he ran on folded wings for a short distance, then rose, flying about the room while uttering shrill, high-pitched cries.

Alec, too, broke his silence, shouting for help as loudly as he could.

The vampire flew from wall to wall seeking escape, then with mouth wide open he went for Alec again. He snapped and bit at the raised broom handle, clinging to it furiously, his hissing sounds filling the cabin.

Alec swung the broom hard against the wall, hoping to smash the bat to death. But the vampire released his hold just in time and flew violently about the room again. Suddenly he found the passageway and was gone.

Alec reached the deck in time to see Henry and the fisherman ward off the vampire with their hats. Then the bat was in full flight, speeding across the open water with the agility and grace of a bird.

"A vampire bat," the fisherman said excitedly.

"You're sure?" Henry asked.

"I've spent too many years in Trinidad not to be sure," the fisherman replied.

"I'm sure, too," Alec said, joining them. "He's the same one we chased from the cave."

"The infected one?" the fisherman asked.

"Yes, the same," Alec answered. "He acted very sick."

"Then good riddance," the fisherman said. "He's

bound for Azul. It's a good place for him. There's nothing there he can feed on."

"I take it we've all changed our minds and aren't staying on the island tonight," Henry said grimly.

"We'll anchor well clear of it," the fisherman said, "where it will be easier to sleep."

"But tomorrow I'd like to come back," Alec said. The island was beautiful silhouetted against the sky.

Shrugging his big shoulders, the fisherman said, "It will be safe enough tomorrow while the vampire sleeps. But tonight we'll stay out to sea, far away from him and these reefs."

The *Night Owl* turned, speeding away in the twilight from Azul Island and the new home of the deadly vampire bat.

Combat!

13

The Black Stallion stood before the end wall, his ears pointed to the south, neighing his song of welcome. No familiar sounds were being carried to him on the air currents but the boy-scent was still very strong. His nostrils searched the wind for further clues as to distance and time separating him from the one he loved.

For a long while he remained still, patiently waiting. Then, as the last patch of sunlight cast a brilliant sheen on his muscles, he snorted uneasily, for the upwind scent was growing faint in his nostrils. The canyon grew darker in the deepening twilight. Still he waited, his patience tried, his anger mounting.

There came the moment when the air carried no wind-borne stimulus and only anger was left within him. Whirling away from the high yellow wall of stone, he went to the center of the canyon. Furiously he reached down to graze, pulling up roots and earth with the grass, snatching wildly and glancing up from time to time with tufts and sticks protruding from the corners of his mouth.

With the boy-scent gone, his thoughts turned quickly to the mares he had forsaken. Snorting once more, he wheeled and left the canyon, his loud whistle shattering the stillness of early evening.

He found his mares with the herd, grazing content-edly beside the pool. Again he shrilled his challenge, expecting mares and stallions alike to cower in terror at the sight of him. But aside from a quick raising of heads there was no movement. Tall and long-limbed he ran through the cane, his steady, easy gait un-changing.

The red stallion awaited the black challenger. He stood before his herd, his proud head raised high, watching the Black approach as if he had long anticipated the other's return. He was not frightened by his enemy, only wary and cautious, for he knew him to be a worthy opponent.

Suddenly he uttered his first sound—a snort, followed by a loud, sharp whinny. Behind him his herd stopped grazing to form a tight ring, the mares and foals in the center and the young stallions on the outer edges. Then the red stallion moved forward slowly as if content to have the fight brought to him.

The Black swept through the growing darkness, his

hoofs beating rhythmically. He was as cool and as confident as the horse who awaited him. But he was not rushing headlong into the encounter and his gait slowed when he reached the short, thick grass of the valley floor. His eyes grew brighter as the herd stallion moved forward to meet him.

There was little difference between the two stallions. Each was a king in his own right. Each was beautiful and powerful to see. They moved toward each other, their strides now of equal length, their small, arrogant heads held high. Closer and closer they came to a fight that could only end in the death of one! Their speed increased as the distance lessened between them. Then at the moment of contact they screamed in unison, their heads no longer held high but thrust out as pointedly as snakes'. On winged hoofs they lunged at each other, their bodies clashing while bared angry teeth sought a hold.

The high walls of the valley picked up the sound of the impact made by their powerful bodies and hurled it back into the arena. After their first terrible encounter they fell back, each more wary than ever and searching for an opening. Equally fast on their feet, they feinted skillfully with thrashing legs. Again they fell back, waiting for an opportunity to strike and respecting each other's superb fighting skill.

Slowly they made a large circle around one another, each looking for an opening to leap at the other's neck. Neither had inflicted serious injury despite their first furious encounter. They strode nobly, heads up, eyes dilated, their nostrils flaring.

There was no hurry in their movements. Each had the patience of a born leader and was waiting for the other to drop his guard. They continued to move in circles. They strutted and snorted. They smelled each other and the wind. And as they kept walking their nostrils suddenly quickened to a new scent on the upwind! It was only a faint whiff but irritating enough to cause them to take their eyes off each other.

Simultaneously they turned to the herd and the cliffs beyond. It was as if they had forgotten their fighting for the moment in the face of a still greater danger.

The sky was clear and the first stars were beginning to appear. The breeze grew stronger with the coming night, riffling the manes of the stallions. As the new scent became more powerful and unpleasant, the two stallions moved forward, not toward each other but in the direction of the herd. They moved almost as a team, sniffing the upwind.

Then they saw the source of the heavy, sweetish scent and snorted loudly. Their signal of danger sent the herd screaming and tearing down the valley in full flight. The two stallions reared skyward as if trying to reach the vampire bat that flew directly at them! Together they smelled sickness and death in its attack.

The vampire glided overhead and the stallions sought to grab it with their teeth and beat it with their forefeet. Missing, they made a lightning turn, streaking with the bat down the valley. Far beyond them raced the herd, the mares screaming as if they would never stop.

Both stallions ran wild, their hatred and fear of each other gone in the face of the winged death that swept just before them. They followed the ghostly black phantom as it floated through the dim murky veil of the oncoming night. With great strides and extended heads they sought to overtake the vampire. Neither stallion had reached the limit of his speed but both were quickly rising to it. Each meant to run down the vampire and kill it lest it escape and return quietly in the night.

The Black screamed and surged forward at greater speed. The red stallion's straining body rose and fell beside him, following the vampire's flight. Then the red stallion uttered a terrifying blast and for a moment he gathered himself as if to turn upon the Black. But instead he leveled out still more, keeping abreast of the other. Stride for stride they thundered, straining for every bit of speed in them. Neck and neck, the two stallions raced after the vampire, their nostrils filled with the smell of disease and death.

As they swept toward the tall cane, the Black was ahead for a few strides. But the red stallion pulled up quickly, and once more the two horses raced as one, gaining rapidly on the vampire. Together they swept into the cane with a new and electrifying burst of speed that sent the stalks flying apart. Every muscle was strained to the utmost as they followed the erratic flight of the bat. But just as they drew alongside it and sought to reach it with raking teeth, the vampire rose high, turned and swept back toward the herd.

Terrified, they went after it, their strides lengthening until they, too, seemed to be flying. When they left the cane their hoofs were pounding out a thunderous rhythm that silenced the whir of wings in the night. Like phantom shadows they swept after the vampire.

The red stallion uttered a shrill cry of warning to his herd, and responded to it himself with a terrific burst of speed. Out in front of the Black he swept, racing alone after the vampire bat!

The Black Stallion stumbled, recovered and picked up stride again, his great body stretched out to still greater length. He had lost a little ground and quickly tried to make it up. Stride for stride, he moved in the red stallion's wake. Then slowly, ever so slowly, he began narrowing the gap between them.

The big herd had wheeled in a closely knit pack of surging heads and bodies and was running up the valley. The very ground rocked with the beat of their hoofs and the air was filled with their screams. Desperately they tried to lose their winged pursuer.

The two stallions turned up the valley, the Black saving ground on the inside and pulling up alongside the red stallion. Head and head they bobbed as one. Eye and eye. Both kept going. Each took up the other's challenge, met it, staved it off and went on.

The vampire bat darted before them, flying erratically up and down but always in the direction of the running herd.

They sought to seize it with their teeth, toss it to

the ground and stamp it to death. Their sensitive nostrils were filled with its unpleasant smell. The sweetish odor drove them insane with fury—and fear, too, for sickness was heavy in the wind!

The herd swept to the far side of the valley, the mares becoming more panicky than ever as the vampire bat neared them. They screamed louder, bawling at their foals and galloping around them until the ground shook with the sound. They bumped into one another, some of them falling but quickly regaining their feet.

Still head to head, racing as a team of equal size and stride, the two stallions swept after the bat. Winging across the valley, snorting in rage and frustration, they sought to run down the vampire before it reached the herd.

The red stallion swerved to the right, following a sudden turn made by the bat. He shook his head, fighting to keep his balance. The Black slid into the sharp turn with him, picking up stride and moving alongside, and the two followed the bat as it swept away from the herd. Now there was only the long stretch of valley before them, and both stallions leaped forward as if all their energy had been released at once. The wind whistled in their pointed ears as the gap between them and the vampire closed rapidly.

Suddenly the Black began pulling away from the other horse and his ears flicked back from time to time as if he were listening to the hoofs behind him. Faster and faster he surged forward.

The red stallion took up the challenge, his enormous strides making it seem that he had been simply loping along before. He inched up to the Black until once again their sleek bodies raced as one.

Together they swept down the valley with the speed of winged thunderbirds in full and awesome flight. They flew into another sharp turn close to the bat, but their speed carried them too wide of the mark and they lost ground to their enemy. Eagerly they jumped back into full stride again.

The vampire headed once more toward the herd and, snorting, the two stallions followed it. This race was not like any other race. It was not simply a case of one horse finishing in front of another horse. This was a race of life and death, and their instincts drove them onward to protect the herd, for their nostrils told them more than their eyes could see.

By this time, although their long strides were still steady, they did not come quite so effortlessly as before. Their supreme speed was being wrung out of sheer stamina and the pace was beginning to tell on both stallions. Yet neither checked his sustained drive, for neither lacked heart or courage. As they raced across the walled arena, going all-out, they began to experience the pain of spent horses.

Laboriously the Black drew inches ahead. But the red stallion was not to be left behind. He skimmed closer to the ground, slowly winning back the margin the Black held over him. Together they cut down the vampire's lead. But the bat was rapidly overtaking the exhausted herd and would reach it within seconds!

The stallions surged forward together, their breath and strides coming hard. Again they inched closer to the winged killer which was now hovering above the herd. Head and head, nose and nose, they began their final drive. There was a tremendous surge of bodies as they jumped forward together, bursting into the center of the herd with their teeth reaching for the vampire!

One mare was down on the ground with the bat directly above her. She rolled over on her back and started to kick wildly with all fours, neighing in terror at the same time. The vampire circled but didn't attack.

After the bat went the two stallions, thrashing the air with thunderous hoofs. They streaked through the herd, rearing up from time to time and showing their bellies to the sky. They flung themselves at the vampire, seeking to tear it to pieces.

Breathing heavily, the red stallion plunged down from his full rearing height. He stumbled and fell, but quickly managed to get to his feet. Again he raced back and forth, following the erratic flight of the bat.

The Black had gathered all four legs beneath him and was vaulting into space. For a second it looked as if he had struck the vampire. But he missed the bat and came down hard, just managing to keep his balance. For a few seconds he stood perfectly still, his ears pitched forward, ready to attack again. He snorted his frustration when he saw the vampire dart away.

COMBAT!

The red stallion spun quickl_
thrashing the air, struck the bat a g_
vampire flew over him. But he did no_
ground; it darted high above the herd an_
toward the cliffs.

The two stallions stood alongside each other quietly, knowing that for a while danger to them and the
herd was over. Together they would maintain a vigil
throughout the night. They were terribly tired but
their breathing was regular once more and came
without effort. Soon the vampire would attack again
and they must be rested and ready for him.

Winged Death

14

The vampire bat hung head downward, dangling over the cliff's edge into space. He had one hind claw hooked onto the jagged stone and his belly had a silvery gray sheen in the moonlight. It was a very small stomach, especially designed by Nature to take only blood as food. Nature also had adapted his teeth to his need, providing him with sharp and curved front ones which were excellent for lancing and scooping. The wound he made was always shallow, small and clean-cut.

He could see the horses below, for contrary to common belief his vision was good if not excellent. It was only a question of time before he would strike again. His small eyes followed the movements of the two stallions whom he now feared. Normally his only enemy was the night owl. He lived a peaceful life, sleeping during the day and becoming active only at night when he went off in search of food. Normally, too, his bite was harmless, producing no pain and seldom weakening his victim from loss of blood.

Suddenly he dropped from his perch with outspread wings and hung suspended in the air for a moment. Then he returned to the ledge, walked along it slowly on folded wings and went to a crevice in the wall. He backed into it in mouselike fashion and for a few minutes was very still, seemingly close to sleep. This complete relaxation was not normal. Neither was the saliva that appeared on his lips. Both were characteristic of his diseased condition.

He felt sudden tremors within him and then a growing irritation began to fill his small body. Fearing the two stallions below, he sought to quell the gnawing urge to attack so soon. He backed further into the crevice where he would be safe and secure.

It was thirty-one days since rabies had been transmitted to the vampire bat from diseased cattle in Trinidad, and during all that time the deadly virus had been present in his salivary glands. Yet only now was he beginning to show the *visible* effects of the disease he carried. They foretold his own fast-approaching death.

For a long while he remained still. Heavy clouds blanketed the moon and the night grew ink-black. Often he uttered a sharp cry, too high-pitched for even wild horses to hear. He listened to the sound vibrations which told him better than his eyes could how close he was to objects about him and, equally important, what they were.

As the hours went on he became more irritable and impatient, further signs of his ever-spreading infection. Finally, the drive within him turned to aggressiveness and he was no longer able to quell his mounting excitement. He left the crevice.

As he looked down from the ledge he could not see the horses but he knew that they were still there. He turned his head from side to side, almost as if shaking it. His cries suddenly changed, becoming peculiarly piercing shrieks as if he had been swept into a state of extreme terror. His mouth hung open, while violent muscular tremors racked his small body. He made no attempt to fly, only staring below and squealing continually.

When finally he did move there was no evidence of any incoordination or paralysis having set in. He walked quickly along the ledge, only to stop at the end and hang from one hind leg while grinning and uttering hissing cries. A few minutes later he was back on his feet, snarling viciously. He snapped at the stone wall and flew violently at it, lacerating his face and wings in his crazed frenzy. He gnawed the air with a hissing sound, then darted for the crevice again. A moment later he emerged from it and hung down once more from the ledge, staring fixedly below.

The two stallions stood on guard, as motionless as statues, clean in line from ears to hoofs. But suddenly,

as if at a signal known only to themselves, they moved
against the night wind, trotting slowly in front of the
herd, one going to the right, the other to the left.
They traveled so smoothly they seemed to glide
through the night, even their hoofs failing to break the
silence. They might have been from another world,
crossing empty space.

Like the vampire bat they were at home in the
night. Their eyes swept the darkness, but even more
trustworthy were their nostrils and ears. Sharp vibrations caused sudden movement of the skin across their
eardrums. The clicks meant danger was near. Anxiously they turned to the herd. Only the foals were
down on the ground, sleeping. All the others were on
their feet, standing quite rigid and occasionally snorting in fear and apprehension. A few brave mares
grazed, ignoring the sounds and smells of the night
and leaving it to their leaders to protect them.

An hour passed before there was a change in the
scent carried by the wind. The two stallions searched
it desperately for minute clues, smelling and listening
and finding it clear of all danger. Had they nothing
more to fear or had their deadly enemy merely gone
downwind?

Blowing down their nostrils, they moved toward
one another, not to fight but to smell each other.
Close together they moved in a small circle, swinging
their bodies away from each other and smelling hard.
Their ears were cocked downwind and yet they knew
their enemy could be quite close without their hearing

him. On signal they separated, the red herd-leader moving downwind while the Black remained where he was.

When their instincts told them the dreaded vampire hadn't left the valley, they became more alert and watchful than ever. Neither would sleep or relax his vigil, for the hours to come were fraught with danger.

The night became blacker still with a heavy, rolling overcast descending upon the valley. There was a chilling dampness to the air, too, forecasting the drenching rain to come. The mares began to graze, no longer smelling danger. Nor did they stop when without further warning the rain came down heavily. They seemed to welcome its rawness, some even lifting their heads to the sky to let the big drops slap hard against their faces. Finally the rain stopped and the night was still again except for the cold currents of air sweeping across the valley.

The two stallions waited silently, ghostly shadows in the night. Another hour passed. It was the period just before daylight, and the horses in the herd began to sleep, most of them still standing up.

One old mare, standing on the outer fringes of the herd, got down beside her sleeping colt. She, too, was tired for she was heavy again with foal. She closed her eyes and slept but, like the other wild ones, kept her nostrils and ears alert.

The vampire bat landed downwind where the old mare could not smell or hear him. On folded wings he walked toward her, slowly, cautiously. He was very hungry, not having eaten in forty-eight hours.

Step by step he moved forward on all fours. He kept his wings close to his body in umbrella-like fashion, giving his forelegs more freedom of movement in case of alarm. No one heard him, not even the two stallions on guard.

Closer and closer he approached the old mare, stalking more lightly than ever by raising his body higher from the ground. From this position, too, he could leap upward and take flight if necessary. He kept his head down yet every movement was planned, deliberate. His wings were so compactly held that no one would have taken him for anything but an agile four-footed animal. He moved softer still, almost prowling, as if looking for the most perfect spot to approach his prey without awakening her.

Reaching the mare, he stalked back and forth as if still undecided which area to bite.

Suddenly the mare showed signs of movement and the bat froze. Nodding his head, he drew back his lips, exposing the large canines and protruding incisor teeth. His gaze never left the mare, and he made no attempt to flee. Instead he patiently waited until she was quiet again. He was extremely cautious in his next approach, keeping well out of reach of the mare's hoofs. One blow from them could easily kill him. He moved forward inch by inch.

The mare made another abrupt movement with her legs and the vampire hopped backward. He waited several minutes before resuming his attack. Then, feeling his way forward, he squatted and leaped, landing softly on the mare's shoulder.

The old mare smelled him before she felt his touch. Rolling over on her back, she started kicking with all fours, at the same time screaming wildly. Again and again she struck out, not knowing exactly where her enemy was and hoping to scare him away. Beside her stood her colt, trembling with fear of the unknown and staring into the darkness.

The red stallion came from a short distance away, the maddening smell of the bat once more in his nostrils. He screamed as wildly as the mare toward whom he rushed. He could not see his winged enemy but he knew that it was somewhere nearby.

As he listened to the squealing mare and colt, he became insane with fury. Suddenly he saw the bat on the ground before him and plunged forward.

The vampire hopped away, his head shaking from side to side. Then, as the red stallion's hoofs reached to stomp out his life, he was in the air. He had no thought of fleeing, only of attaching himself to the stallion's back where he would hang on like a tick. He hovered above the legs that pawed the air in search of him. He was more agile than his opponent and had the advantage of flight.

He circled, ready to strike again. His eyes were bright with the sickness that was blinding him more than the night. He uttered sharp cries which guided his flight away from the high wall and back to the stallion. And then his cries changed with the ever-

growing infection within him. He shrieked in terror
and then dropped to the ground, his mouth wide open
and his head turning from side to side. He waited until
the stallion's hoofs were almost on top of him before
rising again, more slowly this time, as if paralysis were
already setting in. He snarled viciously and flew just
above the pawing hoofs, snapping at them in his
crazed frenzy.

The red stallion struck out hard, moving forward on
his hind legs. He followed the quick erratic flight of
his enemy, side-stepping with him as the bat darted in
all directions and lunging repeatedly. The stallion was
lightning and dynamite rolled into one. But for all his
agility and skill he could not strike the vampire. Once
he pitched forward hard, his head almost striking the
ground. For a second he lost his balance, stumbled
over a large tuft of grass and fell easily, rolling over on
his side.

Before he could get up the vampire was on his neck,
seeking to hold on with his sharp hind claws. The red
stallion struggled to his feet, shaking his great body,
but he could not rid himself of the bat. Screaming in
hatred and terror he plunged forward, flaying the air
with his hind legs. Failing to loosen the bat's claws, he
then reared up on his hind legs time and time again,
coming down with his head between his forelegs. Still
the vampire clung to him. But the red stallion would
not admit defeat. He threw himself to the ground,
breathing heavily and consumed with rage. He rolled
over, struggling to loosen his foe's grip.

The vampire waited for his victim to become exhausted and cease struggling; then he would inflict his wound. His eyes shone wildly, his hissing never ended. He was excited, impatient.

Suddenly, like a panther the Black Stallion struck from out of the night. He too had come quickly, quietly when the mare began screaming. But just before the fight began instinct told him it was not yet time to attack such an elusive quarry. It was only when the vampire ceased flying and attached itself to the red stallion and the two went down that the Black charged with the speed of forked lightning. He grabbed the vampire by its outstretched wings, shaking it loose from the other stallion, and flung it to the ground.

Then he struck hard, using both forefeet, until the enemy was dead.

Dangerous Waters

15

Alec lay in his bunk and listened to the swells slapping ceaselessly against the hull of the anchored boat. He stared blankly into the darkness of the cabin before glancing once again at the open porthole. Soon the sky would be touched with pale gray streaks. Soon it would be morning and he could go looking for his horse again.

Henry snored across the way from him. And up on deck he could hear the captain's footsteps. Yes, soon it would be light and the *Night Owl* would no longer lie restlessly like himself, straining her anchor mooring with the ocean swells. He closed his eyes again, waiting impatiently for the dawn. The smell of the sea was strong in his nostrils—salt and iodine and fish. A big, recently used net hung close beside his bunk. His thoughts turned to home and to the more familiar scents of hay and grain, saddle soap and leather. Would he return with his horse? Or would he have to travel back alone?

He opened his eyes. The footsteps on deck had ceased. So had Henry's snoring and the soft slapping of the waves. But now, mixed with the smells of the sea, was the familiar aroma of coffee. The dead silence all around was of the kind that precedes dawn. Alec got to his knees and looked out the porthole. The pale gray streaks were there, low in the east. As he watched they rose a little higher in the sky. Shadowy waves lifted and rolled toward him, gently rocking the boat.

He heard the fisherman's footsteps again, this time thumping down the steep companionway. Then from the galley in the stern of the cabin came the clatter of dishes and stronger still the aroma of freshly made coffee.

Alec swung out of his bed and dressed quickly. He leaned across the passageway, shaking Henry. "Breakfast," he prodded. "C'mon, get up." His old friend stirred, grunted, opened his eyes and closed them again. "Come and get it," Alec prodded again.

Henry turned over. He didn't seem to have heard.

"Coffee's ready," Alec said more cheerily.

Henry's eyes opened. "Coffee? Did I hear you say coffee?" He wrinkled his large nose, sniffing appreciatively, then turned over on his back. "I'm up," he said.

Alec went down the passageway but stopped outside the galley. It was small, furnished with a small stove, a small sink, a small icebox, and at the moment was occupied by their very large skipper.

"How about some breakfast?" the man asked.

"Sounds good."

"Eggs fried?"

Alec said, "Fine." The boat lurched and he spread his feet farther apart to keep his balance.

"Your friend?" the skipper inquired, busy at the stove.

"Up," Alec answered. "The coffee got to him."

A few moments later Henry joined them. Through the small porthole above the stove they could see the mounting grayness. The ocean swells struck a little harder against their prow.

"What's it like upstairs?" Henry asked, finishing his coffee.

"Looks good, boss," the fisherman answered.

Later they left the pans and dishes piled high in the sink and climbed the ladder to the deck. The boat was pitching a little more and the stern was low in the water. They stood with legs wide apart, balancing themselves and watching the sun pierce a hole in the dawn's gray curtain. An equally impressive sight was the towering dome of Azul Island, already gleaming in the pale, early light.

"There she stands," Henry said jovially, but there was an undercurrent of awe, too, in his voice.

The fisherman started the engine, bringing life to

the *Night Owl* with a rhythmic throbbing. But he didn't put the boat in gear. Instead he turned with the others to look at the rugged shoreline three miles away across the even, untroubled sea. The black cliffs of Azul Island looked ominous, contrasting sharply with the glowing dome.

"In this light it looks more like a medieval castle than ever," Alec said.

"A fortress, you mean," Henry said.

"Except for the swell beach," Alec agreed.

Their eyes turned to the clean strip of sand, so bright in the sun. They watched the surf roll high upon it, then ebb back into the sea.

"It's only a small part of this island," Henry mused. He turned to the skipper, his eyes disbelieving. "You're sure . . ."

The big man at the wheel smiled. "We're very sure, boss. There's nothing inhabitable on Azul Island except the spit. Others before you have been curious. The rest of it is nothing but rock, solid rock." The smile left his face. "Perhaps it is best to leave it alone and go on to one of the other islands."

"No," Alec said quickly. "We'd decided to land."

"But you can see 'most all of the spit from the boat," the fisherman answered, concern creeping into his voice.

Alec studied the big man's face. Why didn't the skipper want them to land there?

"The vampire is there," the fisherman said as if reading Alec's thoughts.

"But he'll be asleep," Alec pointed out. "We decided it would be safe to land during the day."

The fisherman nodded his head. "Yes, we agreed to that. But during the night I was thinking about the way he attacked us. I know from what I have seen of the vampire in Trinidad that this one does more than carry disease. He is suffering from it himself and is soon to die, otherwise he would not have fought us like he did."

"Then perhaps he is already dead," Henry said hopefully.

"Perhaps, but perhaps not. If he isn't, his sickness will drive him to attack in full daylight as well as at night. No, boss, I do not think it wise to set foot on Azul Island. Maybe in a few days' time, yes, but today, no." He turned away as if as captain he had settled the matter once and for all.

Henry said to Alec, "He's right of course, and if the Black was there"—his gaze turned again to the bright beach—"he would have shown himself long ago. You know that as well as I do."

"Yes," Alec said, "but there's the place where the cliffs begin. We can't see that part of the spit from here."

"If he was there he'd be out by now," Henry persisted. "He'd have heard us or picked up our scent. He just wouldn't stay there."

"I know."

"Then let's go," Henry said. "We've got plenty of other islands left to search. And we don't want to get tangled up with any more vampires, sick ones or not."

"Okay," Alec said. "I guess I just felt something extra special about this island."

"Then it's full speed ahead?"

"Yes," Alec said, still looking at the island. "Sure." His gaze left the sandspit for the towering cliffs. Against their darkness he saw a sudden, flashing movement. Then a large black bird rose above the island, its crooked wings and forked tail silhouetted majestically against the clear sky.

The others, too, saw the bird and the fisherman said, "That's strange, a man-o'-war bird nesting here."

"What's so strange about it?" Henry asked, watching the gigantic wings carry the bird toward them.

"He nests only in heavy sea-grape thickets or bushes usually surrounded by cactus. There's none of that here. Azul Island is much too bare for him and his family."

The bird soared overhead, then dropped lower and lower, circling around the vessel time and time again, its bony beak swinging from side to side as it looked down.

Henry grunted and shivered a little as if from cold. "He oughta get along well with the vampire," he said. "Both of 'em are the most devilish-lookin' things I've ever seen."

"I don't think so," Alec siad. "He must be the most graceful flyer in the world."

"You're not lookin' at his head if you think he's pretty," Henry said, his own head crooked skyward, his Adam's apple bulging from his thick neck. He couldn't take his eyes off the long, narrow bill with the horny hook at the end.

"He needs such a bill," the fisherman said. "Like me he depends upon the sea to live. No, I agree with the boy, he is very beautiful, boss."

"He's yours then," Henry said distastefully. "Anyway, let's get going."

The fisherman threw the boat into gear and started to move ahead. The big bird dropped still lower until they could see the small ballooning patch of red skin beneath its neck.

"Wait," Alec said.

"Wait nothing," Henry said. "We're not afraid of him."

"It's not that. I want to watch him. You know, he looks kind of familiar."

"There must be hundreds like him—" Henry stopped, his eyes on the bird again. "Okay," he said impatiently. "Okay, we'll wait."

The *Night Owl* sat on the surface of the water, its motor idling. Over it hung the man-o'-war bird, its marlin-spiked tail trailing loosely in the wind. Suddenly with one stroke of its wings the big bird rose higher into the sky.

They followed its flight, listening to the rhythmic beat of the wings that were like slim, black sails. A short while later the bird hovered above the high dome of Azul Island, soaring, circling.

Henry turned to Alec. "Satisfied?" he asked. "We'd

better get going."

But Alec never took his eyes off the man-o'-war bird. Higher and higher it soared until it was nothing but a black speck in the sky. Finally that, too, disappeared.

"I'd like to go around the island before calling it quits." Alec spoke quietly, his eyes still skyward. "It shouldn't take long."

"No, but . . ." Henry turned to the fisherman, who shrugged his shoulders.

"It's up to you, boss," the skipper said. "At sea I go where you like."

Henry turned back to Alec. "All right," he said. "But let's not get too close. I can think of better places to be shipwrecked."

The faint humming of the idling engines changed to a roar as the *Night Owl* was turned toward Azul Island under a full burst of power. Sharper, too, became the slapping of choppy water against her hull. A wind had come up and the ocean was beginning to roll. Henry growled his disgust as he was thrown against a stanchion. He grabbed hold of it with both hands. The *Night Owl* jumped forward faster still.

Alec braced himself, holding on to the side of the boat while the salty spray washed over his face. Even if the sea got rough, he had no doubt that their skipper could avoid running into the coral rock that lay submerged all around. A lifetime of fishing would have given him the keenness of eye to spot such dangers.

"I see rocks ahead," Henry shouted against the mounting wind.

The man at the wheel only nodded, for he'd already turned the *Night Owl* to starboard, clearly avoiding the submerged coral. As the boat plunged closer to shore the wind grew stronger. They could see waves crashing over rocks that jutted above the surface and sending up geysers of salty foam.

"We're close enough," Henry said nervously. "Give those rocks plenty of room."

Again the fisherman only nodded, for he was turning the wheel, taking the *Night Owl* along the rugged shoreline of Azul Island.

Alec's intent gaze followed the towering cliffs. Exactly what was he looking for, he wondered. It was fantastic to think of his horse being anywhere upon this island of stone. And yet . . . how did he account for the strong feeling within him that the Black was nearby, that sometime soon they would be together again? Certainly not because a big black bird had hovered above this island as if to say, "Stay and look." How ridiculous could a guy get?

The wind blew shoreward, attempting to carry the *Night Owl* with it. Alec braced himself more firmly, his legs straddled as if he were riding the Black at his very wildest. He held on to the rail while the boat pitched and rolled in the surging sea. A strong gust caused the *Night Owl* to lurch upward, the bow coming completely out of the water. He heard Henry shout and turned to see his friend hanging onto the stanchion desperately, his face a greenish-white. The bow came down hard, slapping against the surface with a loud crack.

The man at the wheel edged the *Night Owl* past half-submerged rocks, steering carefully and maneuvering with skill through the biggest waves. He put on full speed when he saw a stretch of smooth water ahead, then slowed down again when jagged rocks pierced the surface, threading his way with caution.

The walls of Azul Island slipped by without a break in them. And to Alec it became more and more evident that the fisherman had been right when he'd said, "*It's nothing but sheer rock . . . and I've been as close as anybody, I guess.*"

The waves crashed over the coral rock, boiling the water with currents and cross-currents and almost hurling the *Night Owl* against the walls. Alec looked across the angry waters at the ominous cliffs and remembered something else the fisherman had said. "*It is best to stay clear of this island. It is only for the devil. . . .*"

Alec glanced at the man at the wheel, then at Henry. If the two of them had had their way they'd have been out of here by now. The fisherman seeing a calm stretch between the breakers, gunned the motor and went through. Then he turned and finding Alec's gaze upon him, asked, "Had enough?"

"We don't need to get so close," Alec answered. "Let's go farther out. Maybe the wind will shift, too."

"It won't shift," the fisherman answered. "It never does."

The *Night Owl* was turned into the wind . . . the wind which swept over its passengers and carried exciting news to the Black Stallion who stood on guard within the walls of Azul Island.

Searcher of the Wind

16

The two stallions stood near each other, identical in size and conformation, equals in courage. Neither appeared ready to fight for supremacy of the herd. It was as if for the time being each was content to respect the other's nobility and right to leadership. How much longer the amicable pact would last only they knew. But end it would—some hour, some day—for there could be only one herd stallion. Meanwhile each was king in his own right.

The Black Stallion nudged some straying colts back into the herd. He disciplined them and reprimanded their mothers for not watching them more closely. He meant to keep the ring intact until he was certain the air was free of all enemies.

The red stallion also remained on guard but unlike his counterpart he had only to utter sharp whistles to maintain discipline. Most members of the herd were well trained to his methods.

There came a moment when the Black Stallion stopped running about in all directions. Wheeling he stood still, watching, listening, smelling. Finally he moved away from the herd, very definitely off guard. Farther and farther down the valley he strayed, his eyes bright, his nostrils quivering. He scented the wind and gloried in the news it carried. He raised his head higher as if seeking to peer over the walls which separated him from the sea. His ears were cocked as he listened intently for some faint, far-off sound. The scent in his dilated nostrils became stronger still as its source drew closer and closer.

The Black trumpeted his shrill call and many of the mares stopped their grazing to look at him. Some stomped their hoofs and neighed in reply but none attempted to break loose from the herd and follow him.

He reared skyward, his excitement mounting and knowing no bounds. No longer did he care to play sentinel to the herd. He dashed this way and that in front of the high walls, his snorts resounding through the valley. Then he turned swiftly away from the herd and headed for the marshlands, his mane and tail streaming gloriously in the wind he created.

He knew perfectly well where he was going and how to get there. His old tracks were not visible on the grassy floor of the valley until he entered the soft marsh. There he slowed down and carefully stepped in the hoofprints he had made before. He wound in and out of the slimy wilderness of tall weeds and swamp ferns, careful to avoid the pits filled with inky water. Only the soft sucking sounds made by his feet in the mud broke the stillness.

He emerged from the marsh and entered the deep gorge that cut through the lower wall of the valley. As before, he was wary of the sharp rocks and boulders along the dry stream bed, finding his way cautiously around them and favoring his bruised foot. But his eagerness to go on was evident in every stride. The wind blew hard in his face, carrying ever-growing excitement and encouragement!

Leaving the twisting gorge, he raced up the tiny valley without so much as hesitating at the stream that crossed it. He cleared it with one magnificent leap, never breaking stride, never slowing in his mad rush to join the boy he loved. Only when he reached the outer wall of the island did he come to a stop, a look of indecision in his eyes.

The wall rose almost a thousand feet, its summit touching the sky and its base split by many narrow crags and chasms. From one opening emerged the stream that fed the small valley, but the Black ignored it. Instead he galloped up and down in front of the wall, shrilling his call to the sea! Faster and faster he ran. Only when white lather covered his body did he come to a stop and seem able to control the fire that burned within him. Finally he lowered his head and put his nose to the stony ground to smell it. Then he walked slowly along the jagged wall, stopping before each of the openings.

At last he found the one he wanted and broke into a trot, following the chasm trail. The high, precipitous cliffs closed in upon him, but he did not slacken his speed. Strong in his ears were the sounds of waves crashing against the outer wall, and more alluring still were the gusts of wind that carried the source of his great excitement.

He slowed to a walk before the tunnel at the end of the chasm but didn't hesitate upon entering it. The light was dim but he had no trouble finding his way. The fine white sand was soft under his feet. The light became brighter as he went along and the wind more gusty. He snorted repeatedly but the sound was deadened by the crashing of the waves just beyond.

He entered the great sea chamber and for the first time fear showed plainly in his eyes. The noise was deafening but even more frightening was the surge of water in the canal. He stood still, neighing repeatedly.

Moment after moment passed and gradually the scent that had brought him there grew fainter in his nostrils. He became frantic, for worse than the fear of the sea was the loss again of the one he loved. Wild with frenzy, he jumped recklessly into the water and swam straight for the opening to the sea.

Outside he found that both the wind and the waves were stronger than when he had swum in these waters

before. He swam farther and farther out to sea,
keeping his head as high as possible, his eyes finding a
distant object that rose and fell with the swells beyond
the reef. He shrilled his call time and time again, and
listened for some faint sound that would let him know
he had been seen or heard. But no such sound came to
him.

He swam more vigorously than ever, carefully
making his way between two pieces of rock whose tips
just broke the surface. Fearlessly he shook off the
waters that poured over him, and kept looking for the
object that beckoned him in the distance.

As the long moments passed the object he was
pursuing became smaller and smaller. And finally he
could no longer see it. Nor was there any wind-borne
stimulus to spur him on. He continued swimming but
only in order to stay afloat.

Finally the Black Stallion stopped fighting and let
the waves carry him back toward shore. There was no
deliberation in his act, only a growing sense of
tiredness and an unwillingness to do further battle
with so formidable an opponent as the sea. He let it
carry him where it would, slowly moving his legs to
stay afloat and to steer him clear of the coral rock in his
path. The instinct to live remained strong and yet
within him grew a sense of indifference as to what lay
ahead.

The wind and sea carried him to the south as well as
back toward Azul Island. And finally the jagged
shoreline gave way abruptly to form the sandspit, its

bright beach jutting out into the water. The Black Stallion let the waves sweep him toward it. He had reached safety but there was no quickening of the blood coursing through his veins, only a deep sense of sadness and loss.

The Quest Ends

17

It was midmorning when the *Night Owl* completed its run around Azul Island and drew opposite the sand-spit again. Alec stood up forward, his eyes on the shoreline, his body wet with the spray that whipped over the bow.

Henry joined the boy. "I guess you'll have to be satisfied he isn't here, Alec. We've done . . ."

A sudden, startled look came over Alec's face. "Give me the binoculars, Henry, quick!"

"But we've . . ."

"Give them to me!" Alec repeated, his voice urgent, demanding, no longer respectful of an old friend. He grabbed the binoculars and hurriedly pressed them against his eyes.

The sky had turned gray and a mist blanketed the

spit of land ahead of them. Alec watched for the movement he thought he'd seen in the ghostly light.

Henry said, "Use your head, Alec. He wouldn't be on the spit. Like I told you before . . ."

"I saw something move! I'm sure of it."

"Maybe it was the bat."

"This was no bat."

"If it was the Black he would have seen us earlier an' come."

Alec kept the binoculars fixed on the sandspit. Finally, he said quietly, "I'm certain he's there, Henry."

"Y'mean you see him?" the old man asked incredulously.

"No, but I will—any second now."

Henry shook his head, more in deep respect than in bewilderment. Alec believed the Black was somewhere on shore and Alec was seldom wrong in the feelings he had about his horse. Again Henry wondered, as he had done so often during the many years of their friendship, just what there was between Alec and the Black. What was there about this boy that made an otherwise untameable stallion submit to him quietly and gently? Whatever it was, it was bringing the two of them together again.

"See him yet?" the old man asked after long moments of silence.

Alec didn't answer and Henry didn't press him. There existed between boy and horse an understanding that was extremely rare in this age of machines and jets and rockets. Henry was more in awe of it than he would have admitted.

Alec suddenly let out a yell that carried sharp and clear across the water. It sent a chill over Henry for never before had he heard such a yell come from Alec. But then, never before had there been such a reunion as this!

For now Henry could see the Black moving through the mist. And Henry surprised himself by letting out a yell almost as loud as Alec's.

The big man at the wheel saw the horse, too, and felt the air become alive with excitement. He turned the *Night Owl* into the wind and went forward at full speed. It would take only a few minutes to round the spit and come in at the pier. Then the boy would be with his horse again.

They met just off the pier, Henry letting Alec go on ahead. The boy did not run to the Black, nor did the Black run to him. They approached each other at a normal, steady pace as if they'd known all along it would end this way. Then they stood side by side, Alec's hands and eyes speaking for him while the Black nuzzled the boy's chest.

Watching them, Henry said, "Skipper, you'd better get ready to carry a lot of horse."

The fisherman nodded, his eyes never leaving the Black. "He's sure that, boss," he answered. "A lot of horse, a whale of a lot of horse."

Moving closer, Henry said, "He's cut up some on the neck and withers. Must be from the coral rock."

"Must be, boss," the big black man agreed.

Henry said, "Walk around him with me . . . slowly now . . . there, that's it. . . . Nothing that looks like the bite of a vampire, is there now?" The old trainer waited anxiously, tensely for an answer.

Finally it came. "No, boss, none at all. Just those cuts on him."

Relieved of tension, Henry said, "That coral rock sure can make pretty bad gashes. Anywhere else an' I'd say he'd been fighting another horse."

The fisherman nodded his big, dark head. "Yeah, boss, anywhere else. No horses here but him."

Suddenly the Black turned from Alec to gaze at the towering cliffs beyond. His eyes shone brightly as he whinnied. Alec listened to the soft, wavering pitch of the call, no different from that which the Black uttered when he scented his broodmares at home.

"What is it, fellow?" Alec looked into the small canyon at the end of the spit.

Henry moved to the boy's side and followed his gaze. "He must have been down there all the time we were offshore. Strange he didn't scent us. Not much gets by him, not usually."

Alec nodded in agreement. He didn't understand it, either, any more than he did the reason for the Black's soft, wavering call which was so strange for this desolate land. But maybe the Black had reasons of his own. They'd have to leave it that way, and anyway nothing mattered except that they were together again.

"We'd better get going," Henry said anxiously. "We don't want to meet up with that vampire again."

"We sure don't," Alec agreed. "C'mon, Black, we're going *home*."

The tall stallion whinnied, this time full of love for the boy at his side. He walked with him toward the *Night Owl*.

Deep within the walls of Azul Island the red herd stallion smelled the wind and the news it carried. Fainter and fainter became the scent of the stallion who had been his equal in fire, speed, endurance and intelligence. But his own passion for freedom had been greater than the other's. He smelled the scent of man and knew where the Black Stallion had gone.

Finally he turned back to his herd. Beautiful in form, majestic in bearing, he looked down upon the young stallions almost in scorn. With large eyes blazing and chest bulging he walked slowly around the herd. Then, as if to get even further attention from mares and stallions alike, he broke into a trot, his mane flashing in the wind, his long tail curving and flowing behind him. He went faster and faster, a red comet gliding across the valley, still the king of an unfallen world!

The others watched their chosen leader and gloried in his strength and courage. They stood motionless while he passed before them, and they trembled a little in reverence and awe. He was the bravest of the brave. And young colts hoped that someday they would be as big and strong as he. Meanwhile, they would graze on the same fine grass as he did, drink the same pure water, breathe the same invigorating air *and always be free!*

The *Night Owl* left Azul Island behind. Standing in the stern was the Black. Once again in his life he had known freedom. His giant body had been cooled by wild winds and rain and warmed by the sun. He had run fresh and clean, his hoofs trimmed by flying rock. His savage instincts had been released and not found wanting. More than ever before he knew that he was all stallion—strong, arrogant and cunning.

The boy at his side spoke to him and he turned to listen to the low-pitched sounds. He whinnied in reply, his nostrils flared to their fullest, his eyes bright. He was greatly loved and he knew it. Nothing else in the world could mean as much to him as the boy's love, not even the freedom of the wild ones. . . .

Slowly he turned his ever-watchful eyes back toward the island. With head held high he surveyed the sea, and suddenly he screamed his shrill clarion call as if claiming the waters for his very own. The air rang with his wild, savage challenge.

A moment later he became stone-still again. Then his wide-open nostrils quivered, followed by a nervous twitching of his ears. He had picked up the faintest whiff of a scent that had sent his blood racing. He had smelled the herd stallion once more.

A sudden gust of wind riffled the Black's mane and tail, and his body rocked slightly with the movement of the boat. Again he whistled his clarion call of battle across the sea.

For a while he had guarded the big herd with all the alertness of the hunted. The mares had looked to him for masterful protection and his faintest signal had sent them racing over the ground. Yes, he had defended them against great danger. He had been fierce in his attentiveness. Yes, he might have stayed and towered above his harem, lord of all he surveyed and wild with freedom except for . . .

He bent his long, graceful neck to the boy again, his nostrils quivering. The sea wind whipped his mane but not a muscle moved beneath his tight skin. He remained still, very still, with his love for the boy showing in his eyes.

Nothing would ever break the ties between them. He had no impulse to return to the island and the wild runners.

"It's over and we're going home," Alec told his horse. "It won't be long now, not long at all."

Alec rubbed the heavily maned neck while the Black uttered a high, bugling snort of joy. And Alec gloried in the beauty of his horse standing so majestically in the morning sun and swishing his tail in perfect contentment.

High in the unbroken sky the man-o'-war bird reappeared and Alec turned to look at it. Why did it stay above the dome of Azul Island? Why had it caused him, too, to stay in these waters when Henry would have gone on? He was making too much of nothing, he knew. And yet . . . try as he would he could not think of this satanic-looking creature as anything but a good omen!

Besides, hadn't it played an important role in his finding the Black again? At least, it had been part of the picture. He wouldn't confide his thoughts to Henry or anyone else; they'd only shrug their shoulders and tell him to stop thinking about what had happened. No, Alec decided it would be much better if he just kept quiet and enjoyed what he shared with the Black—a way of life that was very precious to both of them.

ABOUT THE AUTHOR

Walter Farley's love for horses began when he was a small boy living in Syracuse, New York, and continued as he grew up in New York City, where his family moved. Unlike most city children, he was able to fulfill this love through an uncle who was a professional horseman. Young Walter spent much of his time with this uncle, learning about the different kinds of horse training and the people associated with each.

Walter Farley began to write his first book, *The Black Stallion*, while he was a student at Brooklyn's Erasmus Hall High School and Mercersburg Academy in Pennsylvania. He finished it and had it published while he was still an undergraduate at Columbia University.

The appearance of *The Black Stallion* brought such an enthusiastic response from young readers that Mr. Farley went on to write more stories about the Black, and about other horses as well. He now has twenty-five books to his credit, including his first dog story, *The Great Dane Thor*, and his story of America's greatest thoroughbred, *Man o' War*. His books have been enormously successful in this country, and have also been published in fourteen foreign countries.

When not traveling, Walter Farley and his wife, Rosemary, divide their time between a farm in Pennsylvania and a beach house in Florida.